FABLED LANDS

OVER THE BLOOD-DARK SEA

Dave Morris and Jamie Thomson

Illustrated by Russ Nicholson
Cover painting by Kevin Jenkins

Fabled Lands Publishing

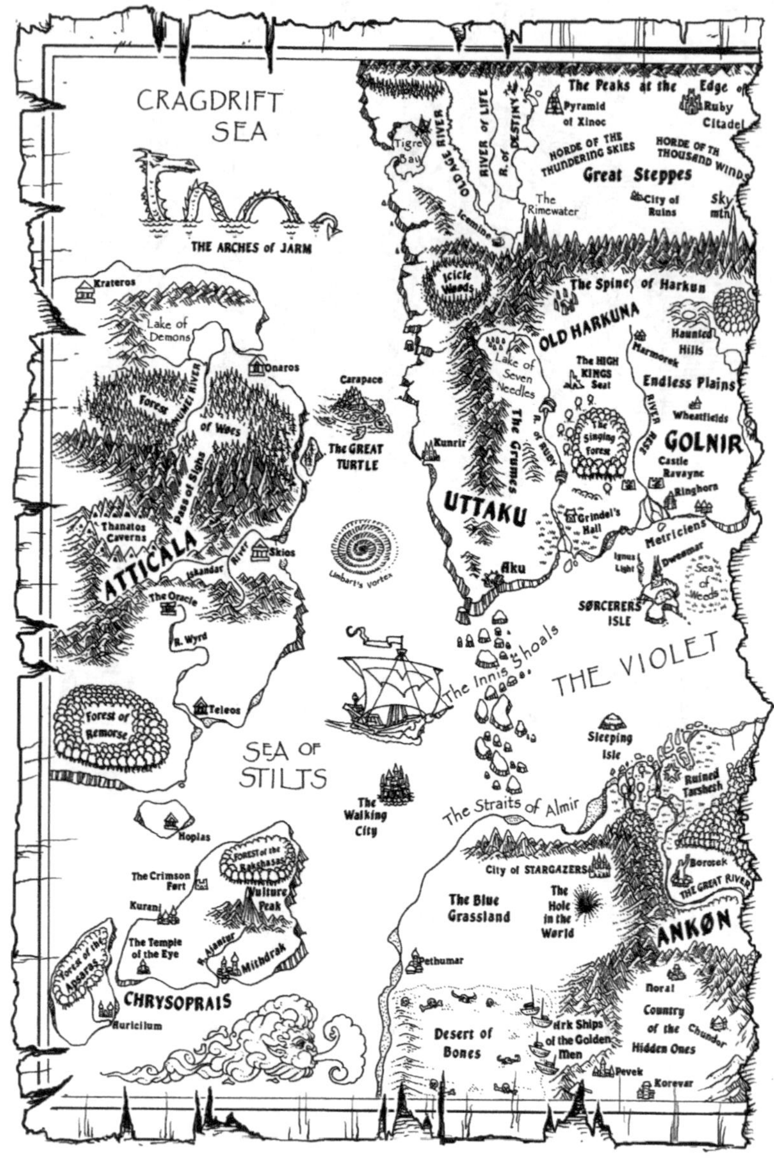

CRAGDRIFT
SEA
THE ARCHES of JARM
The Peaks at the Edge of
Pyramid of Xinoc
Ruby Citadel
RIVER OF LIFE
R. of DESTINY
OLD AGE RIVER
HORDE OF THE THUNDERING SKIES
HORDE OF TH THOUSAND WINDS
Great Steppes
Tigre Bay
The Rimewater
City of Ruins
Sky mtn
Icicle Woods
The Spine of Harkun
Krateros
Lake of Demons
OLD HARKUNA
Haunted Hills
Marmorek
Onaros
Lake of Seven Needles
The HIGH KINGS Seat
Endless Plains
Carapace
Forest of Woes
The Singing forest
Wheatfields
GOLNIR
THE GREAT TURTLE
Kunrir
Castle Ravayne
Ringhorn
Thanatos Caverns
The Grumes
R. of RUBY
RIVER
ATTICALA
R. of RUBY
RIVER
Grindel's Hall
Metriciens
Skios
UTTAKU
Ignus Light
Dwanmar
Sea of Weeds
Iskandar RIVER
Umbart's Vortex
Aku
SØRCERERS ISLE
The Oracle
R. Wyrd
THE VIOLET
The Innis Shoals
Teleos
Sleeping Isle
Forest of Remorse
Ruined Tarsheth
SEA of STILTS
The Walking City
The Straits of Almir
Hoplas
Borosek
FOREST of the Rakshasas
City of STARGAZERS
THE GREAT RIVER
The Crimson Fort
Vulture Peak
The Blue Grassland
The Hole in the World
Kurani
Forest of the Apsaras
The Temple of the Eye
R. Alantur
Mithdrak
ANKØN
Pethumar
Noral
Country of the Chundar
CHRYSOPRAIS
Hidden Ones
Auricilum
Desert of Bones
Ork Ships of the Golden Men
Pevek
Korevar

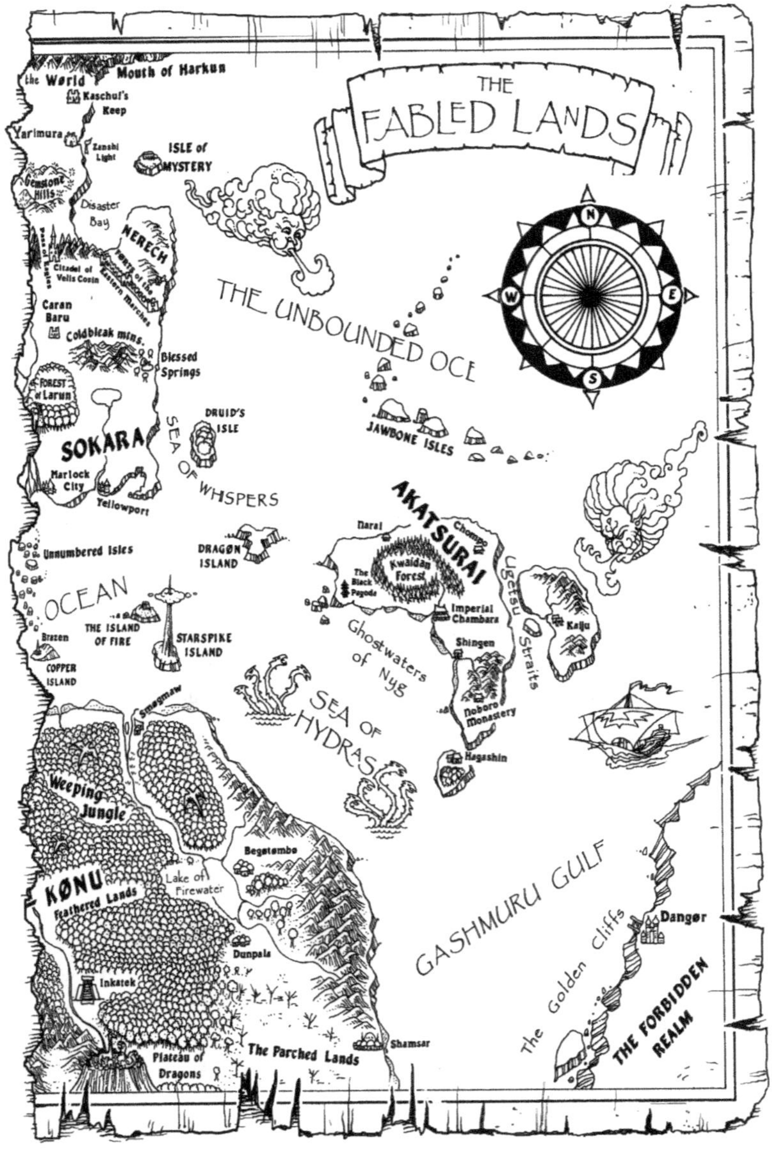

THE FABLED LANDS
the World
Mouth of Harkun
Kaschul's Keep
Yarimura
Zenshi Light
ISLE of MYSTERY
Gemstone Hills
Disaster Bay
NERECH
Citadel of Velis Corin
THE UNBOUNDED OCEAN
N
W E
S
Caran Baru
Coldbleak mtns.
Blessed Springs
FOREST of Larun
DRUID'S ISLE
SOKARA
JAWBONE ISLES
Marlock City
Yellowport
SEA OF WHISPERS
Narai
AKATSURAI
Chombo
Unnumbered Isles
DRAGON ISLAND
Kwaidan Forest
The Black Pagoda
Ugetsu Straits
Kaiju
OCEAN
THE ISLAND OF FIRE
STARSPIKE ISLAND
Imperial Chambara
Shingen
Ghostwaters of Nyg
Brazen
COPPER ISLAND
Snargmaw
Noboro Monastery
SEA OF HYDRAS
Higashin
Weeping Jungle
Begostombo
GASHMURU GULF
KONU
Feathered Lands
Lake of Firewater
Dangor
Dunpala
The Golden Cliffs
Inkatek
THE FORBIDDEN REALM
Plateau of Dragons
The Parched Lands
Shamsar

First published 1996 by Macmillan Publishers Ltd

This edition published 2010 by Fabled Lands Publishing,
an imprint of Fabled Lands LLP

ISBN 978-0-9567372-2-9

Adventuring in the
Fabled Lands

Fabled Lands is unlike any other solo role-playing game. The reason is that you can play the books in any order, coming back to earlier books whenever you wish. You need only one book to start, but by collecting other books in the series you can explore more of this rich fantasy world. Instead of just one single storyline, there are virtually unlimited adventures to be had in the Fabled Lands. All you need is two dice, an eraser and a pencil.

If you have already adventured using other books in the series, you will know your entry point into this book. Turn to that section now.

If this is your first Fabled Lands book, read the rest of the rules before starting at section **1**. You will keep the same adventuring persona throughout the books – starting out as a 3rd Rank wanderer in *Over the Blood-Dark Sea*, but gradually gaining in power, wealth and experience throughout the series.

ABILITIES

You have six abilities. Your initial score in each ability ranges from 1 (low ability) to 7 (a high level of ability). Ability scores will change during your adventure but can never be lower than 1 or higher than 12.

CHARISMA	the knack of befriending people
COMBAT	the skill of fighting
MAGIC	the art of casting spells
SANCTITY	the gift of divine power and wisdom
SCOUTING	the techniques of tracking and wilderness lore
THIEVERY	the talent for stealth and lock picking

PROFESSIONS

Not all adventurers are good at everything. Everyone has some strengths and some weaknesses. Your choice of profession determines your initial scores in the six abilities.

- **Priest:**
  CHARISMA 5, COMBAT 3, MAGIC 4,
  SANCTITY 7, SCOUTING 5, THIEVERY 2
- **Mage:**
  CHARISMA 3, COMBAT 3, MAGIC 7,
  SANCTITY 1, SCOUTING 6, THIEVERY 4
- **Rogue:**
  CHARISMA 6, COMBAT 5, MAGIC 5,
  SANCTITY 2, SCOUTING 3, THIEVERY 7
- **Troubadour:**
  CHARISMA 7, COMBAT 4, MAGIC 5,
  SANCTITY 4, SCOUTING 3, THIEVERY 5
- **Warrior:**
  CHARISMA 4, COMBAT 7, MAGIC 2,
  SANCTITY 5, SCOUTING 4, THIEVERY 5
- **Wayfarer:**
  CHARISMA 3, COMBAT 6, MAGIC 3,
  SANCTITY 4, SCOUTING 7, THIEVERY 5

Fill in the Adventure Sheet at the back of the book with your choice of profession and the ability scores given for that profession.

STAMINA

Stamina is lost when you get hurt. Keep track of your Stamina score throughout your travels and adventures. You must guard against your Stamina score dropping to zero, because if it does you are dead.

Lost Stamina can be recovered by various means, but your Stamina cannot go above its initial score until you advance in Rank.

You start with 16 Stamina points. Record your Stamina in pencil on the Adventure Sheet.

RANK

You start at 3rd Rank, so note this on the Adventure Sheet now. By completing quests and overcoming enemies, you will have the chance to go up in Rank.

You will be told during the course of your adventures when you are entitled to advance in Rank. Characters of higher Rank are tougher, luckier and generally better able to deal with trouble.

Rank	Title
1st	Outcast
2nd	Commoner
3rd	Guildmember
4th	Master/Mistress
5th	Gentleman/Lady
6th	Baron/Baroness
7th	Count/Countess
8th	Earl/Viscountess
9th	Marquis/Marchioness
10th	Duke/Duchess

POSSESSIONS

You can carry up to 12 possessions on your person. All characters begin with 40 Shards in cash and the following possessions, which you can record on your Adventure Sheet: **sword**, **chain mail (Defence +3)**, **map**.

Possessions are always marked in bold text, like this: **gold compass**. Anything marked in this way is an item which can be picked up and added to your list of possessions.

Remember that you are limited to carrying a total of 12 items, so if you get more than this you'll have to cross something off your Adventure Sheet or find somewhere to store extra items. You can carry unlimited sums of money.

DEFENCE

Your Defence score is equal to:
your COMBAT score
plus your Rank
plus the bonus for the armour you're wearing (if any).

Every suit of armour you find will have a Defence bonus listed for it. The higher the bonus, the better the armour. You can carry several suits of armour if you wish – but because you can wear only one at a time, you only get the Defence bonus of the best armour you are carrying.

Write your Defence score on the Adventure Sheet now. To start with it is just your COMBAT score plus 6 (because you are 3rdRank and have +3 armour). Remember to update it if you get better armour or increase in Rank or COMBAT ability.

FIGHTING

When fighting an enemy, roll two dice and add your COMBAT score. You need to roll higher than the enemy's Defence. The amount you roll above the enemy's Defence is the number of Stamina he loses.

If the enemy is now down to zero Stamina then he is defeated. Otherwise he will strike back at you, using the same procedure. If you survive, you then get a chance to attack again, and the battle goes on until one of you is victorious.

Example:

You are a 3rd Rank character with a COMBAT score of 4, and you have to fight a goblin (COMBAT 5, Defence 7, Stamina 6). The fight begins with your attack (you always get first blow unless told otherwise). Suppose you roll 8 on two dice. Adding your COMBAT score gives a total of 12. This is 5 more than the goblin's Defence, so it loses 5 Stamina.

The goblin still has 1 Stamina point left, so it gets to strike back. It rolls 6 on the dice which, added to its COMBAT of 5, gives a total attack score of 11. Suppose you have a chain mail tabard (Defence +2). Your Defence is therefore 9 (=4+3+2), so you lose 2 Stamina and can then attack again.

USING ABILITIES

Fighting is often not the easiest or safest way to tackle a situation. When you get a chance to use one of your other abilities, you will be told the Difficulty of the task. You roll two dice and add your score in the ability, and to succeed in the task you must get higher than the Difficulty.

Example:

You are at the bottom of a cliff. You can use THIEVERY to climb it, and the climb is Difficulty 9. Suppose your THIEVERY score is 4. This means you must roll at least 6 on the dice to make the climb.

CODEWORDS

There is a list of codewords at the back of the book. Sometimes you will be told you have acquired a codeword. When this happens, put a tick in the box next to that codeword. If you later lose the codeword, erase the tick.

The codewords are arranged alphabetically for each book in the series. In this book, for example, all codewords begin with C. This makes it easy to check if you picked up a codeword from a book you played previously. For instance, you might be asked if you have picked up a codeword in a book you have already adventured in. The letter of that codeword will tell you which book to check (e.g. if it begins with A, it is from Book 1: *The War-Torn Kingdom*).

SOME QUESTIONS ANSWERED

How long will my adventures last?
As long as you like! There are many plot strands to follow in the Fabled Lands. Explore wherever you want. Gain wealth, power and prestige. Make friends and foes. Just think of it as real life in a fantasy world. When you need to stop playing, make a note of the entry you are at and later you can just resume at that point.

What happens if I'm killed?
If you had the foresight to arrange a resurrection deal (you'll learn about them later), death might not be the end of your career. Otherwise, you can always start adventuring again with a new persona. If you do, you'll first have to erase all codewords, ticks and money recorded in the book.

What do the maps show?
The map at the back of the book shows the Violet Ocean which is covered by this book. The map at the front shows the whole extent of the known Fabled Lands.

Are some regions of the world more dangerous than others?
Yes. Generally, the closer you are to civilization (the area of Sokara and Golnir covered in the first two books) the easier your adventures will be.

Where can I travel in the Fabled Lands?
Anywhere. If you journey to the edge of the map in this book, you will be guided to another book in the series. (*The War-Torn Kingdom* deals with Sokara, *Cities of Gold and Glory* deals with Golnir, *Over the Blood-Dark Sea* deals with the southern seas and so on.) For example, if you are enslaved by the Uttakin, you will be guided to *The Court of Hidden Faces* **321**, which refers to entry **321** in Book Five.

What if I don't have the next book?
Just turn back. When you do get that book, you can always return and venture onwards.

What should I do when travelling on from one book to the next?
It's very simple. Make a note of the entry you'll be turning to in the new book. Then copy all the information from your Adventure Sheet and Ship's Manifest into the new book. Lastly, erase the Adventure Sheet and Ship's Manifest data in the old book so they will be blank when you return there.

What about codewords?
Codewords report important events in your adventuring life. They

'remember' the places you've been and the people you've met. Do NOT erase codewords when you are passing from one book to another.

Are there any limits on abilities?
Your abilities (COMBAT, etc) can increase up to a maximum of 12. They can never go lower than 1. If you are told to lose a point off an ability which is already at 1, it stays as it is.

Are there any limits on Stamina?
There is no upper limit. Stamina increases each time you go up in Rank. Wounds will reduce your current Stamina, but not your potential (unwounded) score. If Stamina ever goes to zero, you are killed.

Does it matter what type of weapon I have?
When you buy a weapon in a market, you can choose what type of weapon it is (i.e. a sword, spear, etc). The type of weapon is up to you. Price is not affected by the weapon's type, but only by whether it has a COMBAT bonus or not.

Some items give ability bonuses. Are these cumulative?
No. If you already have a set of **lockpicks (THIEVERY +1)** and then acquire **magic lockpicks (THIEVERY +2)**, you don't get a +3 bonus, only +2. Count only the bonus given by your best item for each ability.

Why do I keep going back to entries I've been to?
Many entries describe locations such as a city or castle, so whenever you go back there, you go to the paragraph that corresponds to that place.

How many blessings can I have?
As many as you can get, but never more than one of the same type. You can't have several COMBAT blessings, for instance, but you could have one COMBAT, one THIEVERY and one CHARISMA blessing.

QUICK RULES

To use an ability (COMBAT, THIEVERY, etc), roll two dice and add your score in the ability. To succeed you must roll higher than the Difficulty of the task.

Example: You want to calm down an angry innkeeper. This requires a CHARISMA roll at a Difficulty of 10. Say you have a CHARISMA score of 6. This means that you would have to roll 5 or more on two dice to succeed.

Fighting involves a series of COMBAT rolls. The Difficulty of the roll is equal to the opponent's Defence score. (Your Defence score is equal to your **Rank** + your **armour bonus** + your **COMBAT score**.) The amount you beat the Difficulty by is the number of Stamina points that your opponent loses.

That's pretty much all you need to know. If you have any detailed queries, consult the detailed rules in the preceding pages.

1

You are alone in an open boat waiting for death.

How your life has changed since that day when you set out from your homeland across the Unbounded Ocean! You had signed on aboard a ship with the hope of visiting a dozen ports, seeing a thousand wonders. But calamity overtook your voyage in the first week, when pirates swooped down upon the vessel. You and a handful of shipmates managed to get the cutter down into the water and were making off, but some of the pirates leapt down from the rail right in your midst. The fighting was hard. You remember little of it now, but when it was over the boat was awash with blood and you were the only one left alive. Of your own ship and the pirates' there was no sign – the current had carried you out of sight of any living thing.

Best not to think how you've survived since then. At the mercy of the wind and the currents, you have been swept steadily westwards into regions completely unknown to you. Drinking water has been your biggest problem – you've had to rely on rain, and there has been none for days. Your body is weak, your spirits low. Then, just as death seems ready to draw his boat alongside, you see something that kindles new hope. White clouds. Birds turning high above. The grey hump of land on the horizon!

Steering towards the shore, you feel the cutter lurch as it enters rough water. The wind whips up plumes of spindrift and breakers pound the cliffs. The tiller is yanked out of your hands. The little boat is spun around, out of control, and goes plunging towards the coast.

You leap clear at the last second. There is the snap of timber, the roaring crescendo of the waves – and then silence as you go under. Striking out wildly, you try to swim clear, then suddenly a wave catches you and flings you contemptuously on to the beach.

You are battered and bedraggled, but alive. Now your adventures can begin. Roll two dice.

Score 2-4	turn to **709**
Score 5-6	turn to **505**
Score 7	turn to **714**
Score 8-9	turn to **313**
Score 10-12	turn to **151**

2

You find two important references to the Innis Shoals. The first, in a book on navigation, reads: 'These islands form an effective barrier to the western sea, being ringed with treacherous reefs and racked by constant storms. Only a skilled pilot can bring a ship safely through.'

The other book deals with matters of religion: 'A numinous essence is thought to pervade the air of this region. For this reason, the archipelago has long been accounted as a holy place and many a hermit has made his home here.'

All in all, the Innis Shoals hardly sound the place for a holiday. Unless you're a religious maniac, that is. Turn to **368**.

3

You are sailing a little way south east of Starspike Island, on the edge of the Sea of Hydras.

Go north	turn to **172**
Go south	*The Serpent King's Domain* **300**
Go east	turn to **136**
Go west	turn to **302**
To Starspike Island	turn to **192**

4

A great white bell of canvas stretches overhead, gathering in the wind as a fisherman's net catches a shoal.

'We're making good progress,' observes the helmsman. 'Let's hope this breeze doesn't freshen into a gale, though.'

Roll two dice.

Score 2-6	Storm	turn to **491**
Score 7-12	A safe voyage	turn to **24**

5

You return to the ship and waste no time getting under way. Lose the codeword *Cosy* if you had it.

The helmsman stifles a yawn. 'You know, skipper, I felt quite drowsy on the island,' he says. 'The sea breeze is waking me up, though.'

Steer north	turn to **281**
Steer south	turn to **117**
Steer east	turn to **153**
Steer west	turn to **370**

6

Helpless in the grip of the storm, the vessel cracks apart. The seawater rushes into the broken shell of the hull, dragging you down. The screams of your crewmen are drowned out by the howl of the storm.

Cross off your ship and crew. They are lost for ever. You can think of nothing now but saving yourself.

Roll two dice. If the score is greater than your Rank, you are drowned (turn to **123**). If the score is less than or equal to your Rank, you are swept miraculously towards the shore. Lose 2-12 Stamina points and (if you can survive that) turn to **26**.

7

The stowaway is an assassin who bursts from hiding and runs at you brandishing a long curved knife. 'Nivram the Wizard sends his regards, scum!' he rants.

Assassin, COMBAT 8, Defence 10, Stamina 8

There is nowhere to flee. If you beat him, you can take his **dagger** and the 10 Shards in his purse. Then turn to **78**.

8

The sun is setting by the time you retrace the priest's tracks to a dank cave. A figure in grey robes waits for you. The jewelled rings on his long fingers only serve to make his flesh look still more like ivory.

'I welcome all who land upon my shore,' he says in an eerie drone. 'It matters not to me what port's your home, since now you'll dwell here too forevermore, and feed my veins with blood I'll call my own.'

Panic and anger sends one of the crew mad. He charges up to the cave mouth brandishing his knife. He is only a little fat fellow, and you never thought to hear him utter such screams of hatred. The vampire disembowels him at one stroke, laying him open from gorge to groin. Yellow fat spills out with blood and bile and half-digested breakfast. The vampire laps it all up.

Make a MAGIC roll at a Difficulty of 14.

Successful MAGIC roll	turn to **28**
Failed MAGIC roll	turn to **46**

9

You sail into the coastal waters of Sorcerers' Isle. Here the sea foam takes on an odd pearly glow by moonlight, and strange songs can be heard across the darkling waters.

Put into Dweomer harbour	turn to **152**
Sail around the island	turn to **182**
Steer out on to the open sea	turn to **122**

10

It is getting harder to breathe; lose 3 Stamina points unless you have the codeword *Calcium*. If you survive, you fling open the door to find a large chest containing platinum coins to the value of 400 Shards. 'We got the treasure, now let's be getting out of here!' urges one of your men.

Take a look along the passage	turn to **29**
Return to your ship	turn to **308**

11

Using grapnels you climb with several crewmen to the level of the tunnel. It is jet black, drinking in the sunlight. To explore you must have a **lantern**, **candle** or other light source.

Continue into tunnel	turn to **178**
No source of light	turn to **196**

12

'Lucky it turned out to be pretty old,' remarks the bosun. 'A younger one would have been tough to beat.' Leaning against a tree to get your breath back, you merely throw him a withering glare.

A trail winds up the hillside towards the middle of the island. One of the men sees you glance along it and says, 'Shouldn't we be setting sail, captain?'

Explore further inland	turn to **31**
Return to the ship	turn to **125**

13

Your vessel is more or less due south of Metriciens. The lookout reports no sight of land in any direction.

Steer north		*Cities of Gold and Glory* **210**
Steer south		turn to **504**
Steer east		turn to **402**
Steer west		turn to **200**

14

The ghost resists your best efforts to dispel it. It is intent on returning to its home port of Smogmaw, and its curse means that you cannot put in at any other port on the way. You must now sail directly for Smogmaw; when you get there, the ghost will leave your ship.

Turn to **78**.

15

'What's your game?' says the priestess with a handsome smile.

'Pardon me?'

'Your game.' She fans the cards. 'Maingauche, Black Death, Stake the Vampire… How about Cudgel?'

The two of you play several fiercely contested rounds of the game Cudgel, said to be popular among pit fighters in Trefoille.

Roll two dice.

Score 2-5	Lose 2-12 Shards	turn to **52**
Score 6-7	Lose 1-6 Shards	turn to **52**
Score 8-9	Win 1-6 Shards	turn to **72**
Score 10-12	Win 2-12 Shards	turn to **72**

16

You can take their three **swords** and the 107 Shards they have in their money pouches. One of them also had a **mariner's ruttier** tucked into his breeches; he clearly won't have any use for it now.

When you have finished going over the bodies, delete the codeword *Church* and turn to **44**.

17

A few days out from Smogmaw the *Tidy Sum* is overhauled by your own ship. It is with enormous relief that you see the faces of your loyal lads at the rail.

'Ahoy, you have our skipper!' calls your first mate to the Sokaran captain. `Heave to, if you please.'

The Sokarans don't want a fight. You are paid 150 Shards in compensation and returned to your ship. `A tidy sum,' you remark with a smile to the captain as you leave his vessel.

Note that you are no longer docked at Smogmaw, then turn to **282**.

18

The temple of Badogor is just a hut set in a clearing some distance from town. You enter to be instantly assailed by a horde of cultists whose teeth are as sharp as knife-points.

Make a COMBAT roll at a Difficulty of 17 to fight your way to safety.

Successful COMBAT roll	turn to **37**
Failed COMBAT roll	turn to **123**

19

The crew amuse themselves by throwing apple cores at a shoal of glider crabs. `Look lively, you swabs!' you say to them. `I'll soon find you chores if you're idle.'

They return to their duties with alacrity. `What heading shall I steer, cap'n?' asks the helmsman.

Go west	turn to **630**
Go north	turn to **81**
Go east	turn to **4**
Go south	turn to **227**

20

Did you sell anything at the market that you had previously obtained there for free? If so, turn to **372**. If not, turn to **335**.

21

`Let's steer clear of Uttaku,' suggests the first mate with a fearful glance westwards. `The Uttakin are rank fiends who merely wear the outer guise of men.'

Roll two dice.

Score 2-5	Hags in sieves	turn to **236**
Score 6-7	A fearsome waterspout	turn to **109**
Score 8-12	An uneventful journey	turn to **39**

'A Shard for your thoughts,' you say to the first mate when you find him gazing dourly out across the waves.

'Far to the south, men say, there's a pit that goes right through the world. In its black depths you can see the stars.'

You laugh to make light of his mood. 'Well, what of it? Why so glum?'

'Don't you know the old saying? Battle not with monsters lest ye become a monster; and if you gaze into the abyss, the abyss gazes also into you.' He turns away from the rail. 'What course, captain?'

Go north	turn to **170**
Go south	turn to **79**
Go east	turn to **468**
Go west	turn to **40**

23

One of the crew goes mad and hurls himself from the rigging crying, 'Hydras! Hydras! Cut off a head and two more shall take its place!'

You have his broken body wrapped in a sail and commended to the gods of the sea. Death aboard ship is always a bad omen.

Roll two dice.

Score 2-5	Storm	turn to **83**
Score 6-7	Brooding quiet	turn to **41**
Score 8-10	Haunted	turn to **574**
Score 11-12	A mysterious island	turn to **105**

24

If you have the title Saviour of Vervayens Isle, turn to **169**.

If not, you pore over your charts until late into the night trying to decide where to set your course.

Steer west	turn to **42**
Steer east	turn to **303**
Steer south	turn to **263**
Steer north	turn to **119**

25

If you used a **candle** in the mines, cross it off your Adventure Sheet as it can be used only once. Then turn to **317**.

26

You are swept ashore at the mouth of a wide river. Staggering towards trails of smoke that are rising from beyond a copse of olive-green tropical palms, you arrive at a settlement of many thatched-roofed shacks raised on stilts at the river's edge. It is the depot town of Smogmaw, on the great southern continent. Turn to **44**.

27

The causeway ends in a massive iron door set into the cliff face. It is studded with huge irregular moonstones that look like chunks of frozen milk. You could not possibly open this door on your own.

If you have the codeword *Cosy*, turn to **84**. If not, you must go back, turn to **5**.

28

The vampire speaks in rhyming couplets. Knowing that verse has magic of its own, you realize that you might be able to confound it by replying in the same fashion. Vampires are sly and vicious, but easily baffled.

Attempt to speak in verse   turn to **65**
Try something else   turn to **46**

29

Unless you have the codeword *Calcium*, lose 4 Stamina points because of the difficulty of breathing.

You step into a large dark hold. You eyes have no time to adjust to the gloom before a translucent creature with many frail tentacles comes drifting forward to exude a gobbet of grey vapour in your face.

`Don't breathe it in, captain!' yells one of your men.

Inhale   turn to **47**
Exhale   turn to **67**

30

The closer you get to the uncharted island, the greater your amazement. `Is it a natural island or a man-made thing?' wonders the mate.

You can understand why he's baffled: what lies ahead of you is a disk of jet black marble almost half a kilometre across. It rises to a height of a good hundred metres above the water. From high in the smooth black cliffs, sunlight picks out the edges of a tunnel.

Ascend to the tunnel   turn to **11**
Sail away   turn to **48**

31

You climb up the path, which is gentle at first but gets steadily steeper. It is afternoon before you have reached the peak in the centre of the island. None of your men have had the stamina to keep up, so you are alone as you gaze out over the garden of foliage to where a toy ship crewed by ants bobs gently in a pond.

Three ancient trees stand behind you. With a rustling of long leaves, they seem to speak to you: `If you taste death, it's here you'll be reborn. But heed our warning: three times only can we give you fresh life.'

Cross off any previous arrangements and write Island of Rebirth

(*Over the Blood-Dark Sea* **351**) in the Resurrection box on your Adventure Sheet. If you are killed, turn to **351** in this book. You can have only one resurrection arranged at a time.

The trees fall silent.

You go back to your ship. Turn to **125**.

32

You pore over the charts, reckoning your position to lie dead south of Knucklebones Point.

Head for Sorcerers' Isle	turn to **504**
Steer a course for the Unnumbered Isles	turn to **205**
Head north to the mainland	*Cities of Gold and Glory* **175**
Go eastwards	turn to **77**

33

The crew falls ill. If you have a blessing of Immunity to Disease/Poison, cross it off and turn to **116**.

Otherwise, the ship drifts untended until you are well enough to handle it – by which time you are unknown waters. Roll two dice.

Score 2-4	turn to **58**
Score 5-6	turn to **170**
Score 7	*The Isle of a Thousand Spires* **84**
Score 8-9	turn to **370**
Score 10-12	turn to **40**

34

'What shall we play?' wonders the priestess, pressing the pack of cards against her lower lip. 'Ah yes, how about a sedate game of Paying the Devil?'

She deals the cards. Roll two dice.

Score 2-6	Lose 1-6 Shards	turn to **52**
Score 7	Roll again	
Score 8-12	Win 1-6 Shards	turn to **111**

35

They look up at you with eyes made bleary by drink.

'It's our old skipper,' says Mister Haywood, your erstwhile

midshipman.

'Strike me blind!' says Fryer, once your trusted first mate. 'I never thought to see you this side of hell.'

Threaten them	turn to **53**
Greet them amicably	turn to **130**
Preach at them	turn to **166**

36

You rise rapidly from being an ordinary sailor to the rank of trusty midshipman. Eventually, after many months, the captain agrees to give you your freedom. 'You deserve it,' he says. 'Where shall I put you ashore? How about Old Sokar?' You notice he disdains to use its new name, Marlock City.

Disembark at Copper Island	turn to **99**
Disembark at Dweomer	turn to **100**
Disembark at Old Sokar	*The War-Torn Kingdom* **100**

37

That was one of the hardest fights of your life. Lose 1-6 Stamina.

If you survive, you have the chance to increase your COMBAT score by 1 if you can roll higher than your current score on two dice.

After noting any alterations on your Adventure Sheet, turn to **44**.

38

Perhaps you expected a rugged fellow with arms like anchor cables, but the mine foreman is just a dapper businessman in an ermine robe. He quotes prices for the various goods that interest him. These prices are for entire Cargo Units. You cannot carry this large a quantity in person, but whatever you buy will be loaded on to your ship if you have one docked here.

Cargo	*To buy*	*To sell*
Grain	200 Shards	180 Shards
Metals	575 Shards	550 Shards
Spices	950 Shards	900 Shards
Textiles	250 Shards	220 Shards
Timber	350 Shards	300 Shards

When you have completed your business with the mine foreman,
turn to **317**.

39

You are halfway between the Innis Shoals and Braelak, the Sorcerers'
Isle.

Go west	turn to **58**
Head for the mainland	*The Court of Hidden Faces* **95**
Go east	turn to **129**
Steer south for open ocean	turn to **170**

40

The wind freshens and veers to blow from the north east. You must be
careful, or your ship could be blown on to the reefs fringing the Innis
archipelago. Roll two dice.

Score 2-4	Blown off course	*The Isle of a Thousand Spires* **84**
Score 5-8	A peaceful voyage	turn to **59**
Score 9-12	A vision in the sunset	turn to **551**

41

You are sailing some way off the coast of Ankon-Konu. Exotic Akatsurai
lies far to the north east; strange Dangor, the forbidden city, is to the
south east across Gashmuru Gulf.

Follow the coast west	turn to **337**
Follow the coast east	turn to **60**
Put in towards shore	*The Serpent King's Domain* **400**
Steer due north	turn to **136**
Strike out for Akatsurai	turn to **98**

42

You are in the very middle of the great ocean. Roll two dice.

Score 2-8	Nothing of note	turn to **61**
Score 9-12	A storm brewing	turn to **193**

43

You have not gone far along the avenue before you begin to be
overcome by tiredness. The stone slabs beside the avenue suddenly

look as inviting as feather beds. To stay awake you must either have the codeword *Chill* or succeed in a MAGIC roll of Difficulty 13; otherwise you have to take a nap.

Stay awake	turn to **62**
Fall asleep	turn to **582**

44

Smogmaw is a ramshackle town populated by a human stew of traders, thieves, adventurers, pirates, and fierce natives from upriver. All are drawn here by one common motive – greed. They hope that by trade or crime they will become rich at the expense of others.

You can buy a shack here for 20 Shards. If you do, cross off the money and put a tick in the box next to the shack option.

Visit the market	turn to **86**
Buy or sell cargo	turn to **54**
Go to the quayside	turn to **71**
Enter a tavern	turn to **314**
Return to your shack ☐ (if box ticked)	turn to **74**
Explore the town	turn to **258**
Look for a temple	turn to **128**
Leave Smogmaw	turn to **134**

45

The men rise and stagger back to the beach like narcoleptics. They move as if lead weights were tied to their feet. It is all they can do to keep their eyes open. Only when they emerge from the trees on to the balmy stretch of shore and behold the open sea do they start to recover from their drowsiness.

Turn to **5**.

46

The vampire stands crouched over the body of your poor dead crewman. As the sunlight drains away, it gives an exultant peal of laughter and cries: 'The cooling balm of night anoints the world!'

Attack the fiend	turn to **85**
Drive it off with holy words	turn to **141**

47

Get the codeword *Calcium* if you don't already have it.

The vapour constricts your lungs and throat so that your voice goes up half an octave. Lose 1 CHARISMA point if you are male.

Turn to **67**.

48

You sail away from the strange artificial island. 'Mark it on the charts, mister,' you tell the navigator. If you have the codeword *Callid*, lose it and turn to **717**. Otherwise choose your next heading.

Go south	*The Serpent King's Domain* **100**
Go east	turn to **227**
Go north	turn to **630**
Go west	turn to **153**

49 ☐

If the box above is empty, put a tick in it and turn to **340**. If the box was already ticked, turn to **7**.

50

'The unknown lands,' replies your first mate when you ask him what lies south of here. 'Ankon-Konu.'

Head south	turn to **630**
Head north	turn to **301**
Head west	turn to **9**
Head east	turn to **205**

51

The cabin boy has been found lying in the bilge of the ship with his head bashed in. A belaying pin was found nearby. Possible suspects for the crime include the second mate, who regularly lost money to the lad at dice, and the sailmaster, who was known to dislike him.

How will you deal with the incident?

Accuse the second mate	turn to **536**
Accuse the sailmaster	turn to **707**
Try looking for clues	turn to **499**
Do nothing	turn to **554**

52

The priestess waits to collect her winnings. (Remember to cross the sum off your Adventure Sheet if you do pay.)

Pay her what you owe	turn to **72**
Can't or won't pay	turn to **91**

If you have a ship docked here at Smogmaw, turn to **92**. Otherwise turn to **73**.

Unlike the ramshackle buildings that make up much of the town, the warehouses are stoutly constructed from heavy logs. Not even a spider could squeeze between those mighty timbers — much less even the stealthiest and slipperiest of thieves.

'Spices are the principal commodity of the Feathered Lands,' a merchant tells you. (You must look as if you're just off the boat.) Get the codeword *Catalyst* and then decide what you are going to buy or sell.

Cargo	To buy	To sell
Furs	300 Shards	220 Shards
Grain	250 Shards	200 Shards
Metals	850 Shards	800 Shards
Minerals	750 Shards	700 Shards
Spices	400 Shards	320 Shards
Textiles	250 Shards	200 Shards
Timber	180 Shards	160 Shards

These prices are for entire Cargo Units, which are too much to carry in person and will require a ship for transport. When you have finished your business here, turn to **44**.

55

The weather turns colder. At night there is hoarfrost on the shrouds.
'What lies in these grey waters?' you ask the navigator.

He frowns. 'Mer-folk with tails of hard horn. Creatures like great
scorpions or lobsters, bigger than tar barrels. Spirits of death and cold
moonlight.'

You hold up your hand. 'I get the picture, thank you.'

Roll two dice.

Score 2-8	No encounter	turn to **283**
Score 9-12	A mysterious island	turn to **699**

56 ☐

If the box above is empty, put a tick in it and turn to **75**. If it was already
ticked, turn to **94**.

57 ☐

You put in at an uncharted island. The beach looks a good place to spend
a few days resting under the palm trees while your crew get in supplies
of fruit and fresh water. Restore 1-6 Stamina (the score of one die) if
injured.

If the box above is empty, put a tick in it and turn to **133**. If the box
was already ticked, turn to **171**.

58

A harsh wind rips down out of the north, scattering ice crystals like dust
on the decks.

'Yon wind comes off the far mountains,' says the ship's carpenter, a
widely travelled man. 'This snow may be from the boughs of the Icicle
Woods, or perhaps from the shores of the Rimewater itself.'

He shivers and stamps off below deck to fetch a tot of warm mulled
wine.

Roll two dice.

Score 2-4	A ghost in the rigging	turn to **299**
Score 5-6	Lords of Uttaku	turn to **336**
Score 7-8	Nothing of note	turn to **78**
Score 9-12	An uninvited passenger	turn to **348**

59

At the southern tip of the Innis Shoals lie the Straits of Alvir, by which
you can gain passage to the great western ocean.

Go west through the Shoals	*The Isle of a Thousand Spires* **84**
Steer along the Straits of Alvir	turn to **399**
Go east	turn to **79**
Go north	turn to **96**

60

You reckon your position to be at the southern edge of the Sea of
Hydras. To the south east lies Gashmuru Gulf – and beyond, Dangor
and the Forbidden Realm.

Go south east	*The City in the Clouds* **77**
Go north west	turn to **23**
Go east	*Lords of the Rising Sun* **102**
Go north	turn to **98**
Go south west	*The Serpent King's Domain* **500**

61

An island appears as a dun-coloured smudge hovering mirage-like on
the rim of the sea.

'Copper Island,' says the helmsman. 'Shall I take her into dock,
captain?'

Put in at Copper Island	turn to **553**
Sail on	turn to **19**

62

If you have the codeword *Cosy*, turn to **82**. If not, you can either press
on along the avenue (turn to **102**) or return to the beach (turn to **5**).

63

Several books agree that mermaids can be individually charming, but when encountered in large numbers should be regarded as a grave threat.

'The collective noun is a Threnody of Mermaids,' asserts one source, 'and few who hear their song can resist its dread allure. According to popular belief, a troubadour who learned the song used it to cause all the inhabitants of Gutrein, a town in Old Harkuna, to abandon their homes and follow him. The town remains empty to this day.'

The book goes on to say that mermaids are most frequently encountered to the south of the Ruby River estuary.

Get the codeword *Cynosure* and then turn to **368**.

64

You cannot sail the ship alone, nor would it be wise to venture further inland without your crew to back you up. You go back to the beach, where at least there are provisions enough to sustain you for a few weeks.

A storm hits the island only a few days later. You shelter under the palm trees until morning, when you discover that your fine ship has been wrecked. All you are able to salvage is a broken plank or two. You have rarely been in lower spirits. (Cross the ship off your Ship's Manifest.)

As luck would have it, a mercantile barque puts in at the island before your supplies are quite exhausted.

'We are bound for Ringhorn,' the captain tells you. 'You're welcome to come along.'

Travel with them to Ringhorn	*Cities of Gold and Glory* **2**
Stay on the island	turn to **177**

65

The vampire furrows its bald white brow, perplexed to hear you speaking in verse. It looks like a cat that has caught sight of itself in a mirror. Each time it speaks, you reply with a line that rhymes – and all the time you are slowly retreating down the beach to the rowboat.

Roll two dice. If you are a Troubadour, add your Rank to the result.

Score 2-9	The vampire attacks	turn to **85**
Score 10+	It watches you depart	turn to **41**

66

The sea heaps up. White foam from breaking waves begins to be blown in streaks. 'This is near a gale!' says the mate.

Roll two dice.

Score 2-5	A storm hits	turn to **213**
Score 6-8	The gale blows over	turn to **155**
Score 9-12	Suddenly becalmed	turn to **429**

67

Spluttering, you strike out at the creature but it drifts off into the bowels of the ship. Your two crewmen are so spooked by now that they refuse to stay, and you realize it would be unwise to linger on your own.

Feeling as if hundreds of eyes are watching you through hidden peepholes, you hurry back to the deck.

Lose 4 Stamina points unless you have the codeword *Calcium* and (if still alive) turn to **308**.

68 ☐

The man strides right up to the side of your vessel and hails you as casually as if he were standing on the quayside at Wishport.

If the box above is empty, put a tick in it and turn to **617**. If the box was already ticked, turn to **635**.

69

(If you just ticked the third box, this is your third and final rebirth. Delete the entry in the Resurrection box on your Adventure Sheet.)

You step out of the interior of one of the trees as though emerging from an egg. Your Stamina is back to its normal score, but you have lost any cash and possessions that you were carrying at the time of your death.

Your problem now is how to get off the island. Turn to **177**.

70

The mate's knife flashes — a splash of sticky blood, and the witch falls croaking into the sea to sink like a stone. Something flops to the deck. Her hand. It resembles an old white crab. Note the **witch's hand** on your list of possessions if you decide to keep it, then turn to **39**.

71

If your own ship is docked here, you can set sail – either on to the open ocean or up the wide Nozama river.

Otherwise you will have to buy a ship or pay for passage.

Put to sea	turn to **320**
Sail upriver	*The Serpent King's Domain* **375**
Remain in Smogmaw	turn to **44**
Don't have a ship here	turn to **110**

72

The priestess stretches like a cat, making no effort to stifle a yawn. 'If you'll excuse me, it is time for my siesta.' She lies back on the divan and closes her eyes. You quietly withdraw from the temple. Turn to **44**.

Luckily they are drunk to the point of staggering, and you can fight one after the other instead of all at once.

First Mutineer, COMBAT 6, Defence 9, Stamina 9

Second Mutineer, COMBAT 5, Defence 7, Stamina 5

Third Mutineer, COMBAT 5, Defence 7, Stamina 6

If you try to run off you will be struck a final flurry of blows inflicting 2-12 Stamina points (the score of two dice).

Beat a retreat   turn to **44**

Stay and win   turn to **16**

The shack consists of a bamboo hut raised above the ground on stout poles to protect it from flooding. The roof is palm thatch. It is simple but comfortable.

Each time you return, roll two dice.

Score 2-6   Everything is safe

Score 7-8   A thief has taken any money left here

Score 9-10   Fire has destroyed the shack and its contents

Score 11+   Squatters, turn to **113**

You can rest here if injured (restore your Stamina to its normal unwounded score). You can also leave money and possessions here to save having to carry them around with you. Make a note in the box below of anything you are leaving at the shack.

> *ITEMS IN SHACK*
>
>
>
>
>
>

When you've finished at your shack, turn to **44**. Remember to erase the tick next to the shack option there if your home was destroyed by fire.

75

The bottle contains a **map of Bazalek**, which is a small isle in the waters near Disaster Bay. Make of it what you will. Note the **map of Bazalek** on your Adventure Sheet and, because you may later wish to refer back to the illustration opposite, write *Over the Blood-Dark Sea* **75** in brackets next to it.

Turn to **352**.

76

The girl takes the **heart-shaped locket** and turns, disappearing into the undergrowth. You quickly scramble up the rock and search around, but she has gone leaving no trace.

Your first mate calls to tell you they have loaded the rowboat with fresh water and coconuts. It is time to be off. Remember to record the 450 Shards on your Adventure Sheet, then turn to **171**.

77

The crewmen seem nervous. The Kingdom of the Reavers is not many leagues to the south west, and as a consequence pirates abound in these waters. Roll two dice.

Score 2-6	Pirates as feared	turn to **268**
Score 7-8	Luck is with you	turn to **322**
Score 9-12	Something worse	turn to **437**

78

You are at sea close to the great port city of Aku. Westwards lie the first bleak rocky islands of the Innis Shoals.

Head for Aku	*The Court of Hidden Faces* **200**
Go west	*The Isle of a Thousand Spires* **100**
Go east	turn to **21**
Strike out south	turn to **96**

79

A southerly breeze stirs the sails. Standing at the rail with head tilted back, you bask in the warm sunshine. Is it your imagination, or can you really detect the scent of exotic spices and swaying palm trees carried on the wind?

Roll two dice; add 1 to the roll if you are an initiate of the Three Fortunes.

Score 2-4	Catamarans	turn to **186**
Score 5-6	An electric storm	turn to **168**
Score 7-9	A quiet voyage	turn to **352**
Score 10+	A bottle drifts by	turn to **56**

80

Dead men whose bones are crusted with barnacles creep over the rail at night and carry off half your crewmen. You only discover the cause of the disappearances when you question a sailor who had been locked up in the brig for some minor offence. He saw the barnacle men carrying out their ghastly business through a knothole in the brig door. You have no doubt he's telling the truth; his hair has turned pure white.

Reduce your Crew Quality to poor, then turn to **321**.

81

A strong breeze flutters the sails. The crewmen go about their chores merrily, scrambling through the rigging like carefree monkeys.

'Five bells,' intones the mate.

Recover 1 Stamina point if injured, then roll two dice.

Score 2-5	Pirates	turn to **354**
Score 6-12	An uneventful voyage	turn to **101**

82

The men start to yawn. 'Great gods, I feel sleepy!' announces the bosun, rubbing his eyes.

'Me, too,' agrees the quartermaster. 'Like I'd been poleaxed.'

Despite your stern orders, they go to lie down on the stone slabs.

'Ah, this is a comfy couch,' murmurs the bosun as he shuts his eyes. 'Permit us to take just a quick nap, skipper.'

If you have the codeword *Cerumen*, turn to **323**. If not, turn to **305**.

The sky is the colour of burning sulphur. Thunder rumbles the heavens, making your crewmen quail. 'The wrath of the gods is upon us!' shrieks the bosun. 'Say your final prayers, lads!'

If you have the blessing of Alvir and Valmir, which confers Safety from Storms, you can ignore the storm. Cross off your blessing and turn to **41**.

Otherwise the storm hits with terrible fury. Great grey waves break across the deck. Roll one die if your ship is a barque, two dice if it is a brigantine, three dice if a galleon. Add 1 to the roll if you have an excellent crew; subtract 1 if you have a poor crew.

Score 0-4	Your ship sinks	turn to **103**
Score 5-6	The mast splits	turn to **581**
Score 7-19	You weather the storm	turn to **60**

84 ☐

Lose the codeword *Cosy*.

If the box above is empty, tick it and turn to **104**. If it was already ticked, turn to **433**.

85

The vampire screeches like an angry owl and lashes out with its long white talons.

'Go on, skipper, we're right behind you,' says the first mate nervously.

Vampire, COMBAT 15, Defence 18, Stamina 18

If you retreat to the boat, the vampire will get a final attack as you run off, inflicting 1-6 Stamina points of injury.

Retreat	turn to **41**
Kill the vampire	turn to **195**

Smogmaw market comprises a row of flimsy grass-roofed huts where goods are laid out on straw mats.

Armour	To buy	To sell
Leather (Defence +1)	40 Shards	35 Shards
Ring mail (Defence +2)	150 Shards	100 Shards
Chain mail (Defence +3)	–	150 Shards

Weapons (sword, axe, etc)	To buy	To sell
Without COMBAT bonus	40 Shards	35 Shards
COMBAT bonus +1	200 Shards	175 Shards
COMBAT bonus +2	450 Shards	375 Shards
COMBAT bonus +3	–	750 Shards

Other items	To buy	To sell
Compass (SCOUTING +1)	400 Shards	320 Shards
Cross-staff (SCOUTING +2)	800 Shards	640 Shards
Sextant (SCOUTING +3)	1200 Shards	1000 Shards
Lockpicks (THIEVERY +1)	250 Shards	180 Shards
Mariner's ruttier	–	200 Shards
Selenium ore	–	350 Shards
Holy symbol (SANCTITY +1)	200 Shards	100 Shards
Rope	40 Shards	25 Shards
Lantern	140 Shards	100 Shards
Fretwork key	–	1000 Shards
Parrot	75 Shards	25 Shards
Parrot fungus	150 Shards	120 Shards
Pirate captain's head	–	75 Shards

Items with no purchase price are not available in Smogmaw's market. When you have completed your transactions, turn to **167**.

Lose the codeword *Certain*.

A small boat comes sailing out of a clear horizon. Its single passenger is a bare-chested man in black breeches who leaps aboard with the lithe grace of a big cat.

Challenge the fellow	turn to **235**
Order him seized	turn to **197**
Offer hospitality	turn to **217**

88

There is ample fruit and even a little game, in the form of flightless weasel-birds. The trick lies in knowing what is safe to eat and what is toxic.

Make a SCOUTING roll at a Difficulty of 12.

Successful SCOUTING roll	turn to **144**
Failed SCOUTING roll	turn to **162**

89

The witch promises to mend her ways. 'No more vile hocus pocus for me,' she vows. But the next day she is gone like a ghost, and the helmsman reports that he does not recognize these waters. You have been played for a sucker. Turn to **190**.

90

'I hope you're well-versed in outdoor survival,' mutters an old man, displaying the stump of the leg that he lost to a crocodile.

Follow the coast east	*The Serpent King's Domain* **450**
Follow the coast west	*The Serpent King's Domain* **350**
South west into the jungle	*The Serpent King's Domain* **550**
South east into the jungle	*The Serpent King's Domain* **175**
Follow the riverbank	*The Serpent King's Domain* **275**
Remain in Smogmaw	turn to **44**

91

The gleam that comes suddenly into her eyes, combined with the sweat glistening on her throat, makes her look feverish and wild. 'The goddesses will ensure your account is settled,' she says before sinking wearily back on the divan.

You leave the temple under a curse. From now on you can use only one die when making any ability roll. This curse will last until you visit the temple of the Three Fortunes in Metriciens, whereupon it will be lifted. Note above the Abilities box on your Adventure Sheet: 'Use one die for ability rolls until Three Fortunes temple visited in Metriciens.'

Now turn to **44**.

92

The three mutineers are terrified that you will call your current crewmen to back you up. 'I've got a few barnacles need scraping off my new ship's keel, Mister Burkitt,' you tell your onetime cabin boy with a crooked smile.

He and his shipmates get up quickly. 'Good to see you're well, skipper. No hard feelings, eh?' they mutter, pressing a purse with 40 Shards into your hand.

You watch the three men hurry off. You doubt if you'll see them again. Lose the codeword *Church* and turn to **314**.

93

'Hear that melody, captain?' asks the mate, his expression a mixture of fear and longing. 'It is the song of the mermaids.'

It is an unearthly sound, beautiful but somehow terrible. Men must feel this way when, having drawn their last breath, they gaze on the lovely face of a Valkyrie.

If you have the codeword *Cynosure*, turn to **131**. If not, turn to **149**.

94

The bottle contains a **treasure map**. 'A bloomin' funny thing to find in a bottle,' is all the bosun has to say when he sees it.

The helmsman is more helpful. 'See this stretch of coastline? It might indicate the Sea of Hydras.'

'No,' says the first mate with a dour shake of his head. 'It's the straits near Teleos, I'm sure of it.'

Note the **treasure map** among your possessions and turn to **352**.

95

The girl stamps her foot petulantly and disappears in a thick blast of roiling black smoke.

Note the **heart-shaped locket** on your list of possessions — and remember to record the 450 Shards if you didn't already. Also note the codeword *Citrus*.

You open the locket and immediately there is an unearthly howl and something indistinct flies up past you into the sky. A musty scent hangs in the air. Inside the locket is a picture of a bald man with piercing green eyes.

If you have the codeword *Dangle*, turn to **115**. If not, it is now time to leave the island; turn to **171**.

96

The charts show that you are east of the Innis Shoals, roughly halfway between Uttaku and the great southern continent of Ankon-Konu. Roll two dice.

Score 2-5	Sickness among the crew	turn to **33**
Score 6-9	An uneventful voyage	turn to **116**
Score 10-12	A man walking on the water	turn to **68**

97

The stowaway is a beautiful girl with blue eyes and long golden hair. She tells you her name is Athanasia and she is the daughter of a prince. 'I ran away to sea rather than be married off to my cousin Zolteg, who in many ways resembles a wart-hog,' she explains.

In return for letting her join your crew, she teaches you some lovely songs. Roll two dice and if you score higher than your current CHARISMA, increase it by 1. Turn to **78**.

98

You have reached a torrid clime where the sun beats down mercilessly by day, warping the dry timbers of the ship and turning the ocean into a huge, dark, heaving, fathomless cauldron.

Roll two dice.

Score 2-5	A vessel adrift	turn to **183**
Score 6-8	All's quiet	turn to **118**
Score 9-12	Monsters of the deep	turn to **647**

99

Copper Island is a bleak rocky wilderness. In the lee of the great mountains lies the town of Brazen, a community of dusty slate-roofed houses whose only decoration takes the form of ornamental copper drainpipes.

Visit the market	turn to **297**
Go up to the mines	turn to **317**
Find a tavern	turn to **334**
Look for a temple	turn to **347**
Leave town	turn to **495**

100

You are on a broad platform of polished basalt that extends into the sea. The city of Dweomer lies some way inland, along a paved avenue with stone sentinels on either side.

Put to sea (if you have a ship here)	turn to **122**
Acquire a ship	turn to **406**
Arrange passage to the mainland	turn to **564**
Go along the avenue to Dweomer	turn to **175**

101

'See those myriad islands?' says the navigator, pointing to numerous rocky shores scattered in the west beyond a pall of haze.

You nod. 'The Unnumbered Isles. We're due south of Old Sokar – or Marlock City, as it now is called.'

Go west	turn to **205**
Go east	turn to **119**
Go north	turn to **77**
Go south	turn to **42**

102

With each step your eyelids are getting heavier. You yawn and stretch, feeling utterly weary. Those stone couches look so comfortable.

To stay awake you must either have the codeword *Chill* or succeed in a MAGIC roll of Difficulty 18, otherwise you have to take a nap.

Stay awake	turn to **27**
Fall asleep	turn to **582**

103

Helpless in the grip of the storm, the vessel cracks apart. The seawater rushes into the broken shell of the hull, dragging you down. The screams of your crewmen are drowned out by the howl of the storm. Cross off your ship and crew from the Ship's Manifest; they are lost. You can think of nothing now but saving yourself.

Roll two dice. If the score is greater than your Rank, you are drowned (turn to **123**). If the score is less than or equal to your Rank, you are swept miraculously towards a rocky shore. Lose 2-12 Stamina points and (if you can survive that) turn to **222** in *The Serpent King's Domain*.

104

The combined strength of all your men is just enough to push the iron doors open. Within lies a hidden valley entirely surrounded by high cliffs – a paradise of bubbling brooks, emerald lawns, fruit trees and scented flowers. Strewn all around are gold, silver and gems as plentiful as pebbles in a merchant's garden. With wild cries of delight, your men stuff their pockets with all they can carry.

You yourself pick up jewels worth 5000 Shards. The air here is so clean and fresh that, if wounded, you can restore your Stamina to its normal score. If you were not wounded, you can permanently increase your Stamina by 1-6 points (the roll of one die).

A cold breeze shakes the boughs of the trees. Leaves fall, curling on the grass. 'We've let Time into Paradise,' reckons the mate. 'Let's not linger here.' Turn to **5**.

105 ☐

If the box above is not ticked, tick it now and turn to **338**. If it is already ticked, turn to **159**.

106

The helmsman goes mad in the middle of the night, possibly as a result of smoking tobacco mixed with mauve lotus. By the time anyone notices, he has had plenty of time to work mischief.

Roll a die.

Score 1-2	Lost at sea	turn to **24**
Score 3-4	Out of drinking water	turn to **124**
Score 5-6	Run aground	turn to **212**

107

'Land ahoy!' calls the lookout. It is Fiddler's Green, the island gifted to you by the herald of the sea gods.

| Put in at the island | turn to **143** |
| Sail on | turn to **125** |

108

You tie bundles of saplings together using rope made of plaited palm leaves. Hollow gourds help to provide buoyancy. Commending your soul to the gods, you push the little raft out from shore and climb aboard. It is not so much like sailing as swimming with the aid of a float.

Roll two dice. Add 2 to the roll if you are an initiate of Molhern, god of craftsmen.

Score 2-5	The raft sinks	turn to **123**
Score 6-8	Picked up at sea	turn to **158**
Score 9+	You reach land	turn to **180**

109

An unexplained waterspout erupts from the surface of the sea, carrying your vessel high up into the sky. The sailors cringe in dismay and cling to the rigging for safety.

'Gods above!' cries the cook as he sees the clouds go past. 'We're airborne!'

The mate clutches his throat. 'It's getting hard to breathe...' he says before slumping to the deck.

If you have the codeword *Calcium* you are not affected: turn to **127**. Otherwise turn to **123**.

110

Several skippers have loaded their cargoes and are ready to depart for ports in the north. You can get passage to Dweomer, Yellowport or Metriciens, for 35 Shards in each case. There is also a merchant who intends to go upriver to trade with the natives of the interior; he will take you along for 5 Shards. Alternatively, you could buy a ship of your own.

Pay the fare to Yellowport	turn to **224**
Pay the fare to Dweomer	turn to **242**
Pay the fare to Metriciens	turn to **260**
Accompany the merchant upriver	*The Serpent King's Domain* **475**
Buy a ship	turn to **712**
Stay in Smogmaw	turn to **44**

111

The priestess asks if you wish to become an initiate of the Three Fortunes. You must refuse if you are already an initiate of another temple. If you accept, write The Three Fortunes in the God box on your Adventure Sheet.

Become an initiate	turn to **256**
Turn down her offer and leave	turn to **44**

112

Your former crewmen soon back down when they see two burly natives in feather cloaks and full warpaint getting up to stand beside you.

'This is the friend of Moon of Evening,' says one of the natives, shaking his spear at the frightened mutineers. 'You cause trouble and you will sleep with the piranhas!'

The three hurry off. 'They won't come in here again,' says the other native.

Lose the codeword *Church* and turn to **314**.

113

The squatters cannot see why they shouldn't use your property while you're away at sea. A vigorous two-fisted argument soon sets them straight, but you get a bloody nose and a black eye in the process of evicting them. You throw them in the mud at the side of the river before striding back to your shack. Lose 1-6 Stamina and (if you can survive that) turn to **74**.

114

You are taken before the Reaver King in his grim fortress, which stands at the back of the secluded cove where the pirates have their base. Many a captain in the world's navies would pay dearly to know the location of this place, the secret harbour from which the dread Reavers swoop out to prey on passing ships.

If you have the codeword *Cutlass*, turn to **473**. If not, turn to **233**.

115

The portrait is of your old foe Kaschuv the Deathless. He'll have to choose another soubriquet now you've found and released his soul from the magic locket in which he kept it secure.

The first mate calls to tell you the supplies are stowed aboard. It is time to set sail. Turn to **171**.

116

The mate joins you at the rail and the two of you watch the sun sink beyond the rocky peaks of the Innis archipelago.

'What lies there in the west?' wonders the mate. 'Are you for finding out, skipper? Say the word and I'll set a course for the Sea of Stilts.'

Travel west	*The Isle of a Thousand Spires* **84**
Go south	turn to **40**

| Go north | turn to **58** |
| Head east | turn to **370** |

117

The grey bulk of an island can be seen to the north. 'Why is it called the Sleeping Isle?' you hear the cabin boy ask the first mate.

'Why, lad, it's because a curse puts anyone who goes ashore off to sleep for a hundred years,' is the mate's reply.

Roll two dice.

Score 2-5 A flying horseman	turn to **496**
Score 6-9 An uneventful voyage	turn to **135**
Score 10-12 The Kraken wakes	turn to **465**

118

The lookout spots an island off the starboard bow. Nothing is recorded on the charts for this region, but perhaps that isn't surprising. Few ships return from the dread Sea of Hydras.

| Explore the island | turn to **413** |
| Sail on | turn to **278** |

119

You have a good day's sailing, but at dusk a heavy gloom swathes the sunset in a welter of bloody reds, golds, charcoal grey and livid purple. It looks like a bruise in the western sky.

'Let's hope that's no harbinger of a storm,' says the mate.

Roll two dice.

Score 2-4	Worsening weather	turn to **213**
Score 5-7	A quiet night	turn to **137**
Score 8-12	A ship's lanterns	turn to **533**

120 ☐

If the box above is empty, put a tick in it and turn to **97**. If the box was already ticked, turn to **350**.

121

You look up into two pairs of eyes that glitter like onyx. There is a rustling sound, a snake-like hiss, and then you dimly hear these words:

'This one is stricken like the others, my sister…'

A terrible spell prevents you from moving a muscle. There is a sense of days and nights flitting past in less than a heartbeat. You must summon your fading concentration to shrug off the spell before it is too late.

Make a MAGIC roll at a Difficulty of 14.

Successful MAGIC roll	turn to **713**
Failed MAGIC roll	turn to **522**

122

You are sailing away from Braelak, the Sorcerers' Isle.

Go north	turn to **200**
Go south	turn to **244**
Go east	turn to **504**
Go west	turn to **129**

123

You are dead. If you have a resurrection deal, turn to the section noted on your Adventure Sheet after first erasing your current possessions, money and any details on your Ship's Manifest.

If you don't have a resurrection arranged, this is the end and you can only start afresh with a new character. First make sure to erase all ticks, codewords and Adventure Sheet details in all your Fabled Lands books. You can begin again at **1** in any of the books in the series.

124

With no water in the barrels, you have little hope of surviving to reach dry land. You ask your officers to propose a course of action. The first mate recommends you set course for Dweomer and trust to stringent rationing. The navigator thinks you should circle in these waters looking for an island.

Head for Dweomer	turn to **142**
Search for an island	turn to **160**

125

The sea, which for many days now has been a rich mauve-blue, now begins to take on a rusty colour.

'It is silt from the Nozama estuary,' says the navigator. 'The same stuff that gives Lake Firewater its blood-tinged hue.'

Steer south to Smogmaw	turn to **266**
Steer north	turn to **4**
Steer west	turn to **227**
Steer east	turn to **302**

126

You kneel in the sand for days, eating and drinking nothing, until starvation makes strange visions dance before your eyes. Every moment is spent in prayer. The demands of the flesh are first ignored, then forgotten, as you pin all your hopes for survival on divine intervention.

If you are an initiate of Alvir and Valmir, make a SANCTITY roll at a Difficulty of 17.

If you are not an initiate of Alvir and Valmir, your prayers are completely in vain and finally you give up the attempt: lose 3 Stamina points owing to deprivation.

Successful SANCTITY roll	turn to **198**
Failed SANCTITY roll	turn to **123**
Not an initiate of Alvir and Valmir	turn to **177**

127

The entire ship's company sinks into a coma. Unlike you, they cannot breathe the thin air up here. You must do something before they are all dead.

Use sorcery to save them	turn to **145**
Dive into the sea	turn to **199**
Climb down the side of the ship	turn to **219**

128

You see an old man wading ankle-deep in mud as he crosses from one tavern to another. His reason for not using the boardwalks is that dogs use them too – 'The mud is more sanitary!' he explains.

Regarding your enquiry about Smogmaw's temples, he mentions four: 'There is the shrine to Alvir and Valmir, the temple of the Three Fortunes, a shrine to Glimbinki the Plumed One, and somewhere there's a fane sacred to Badogor.'

`Who?'

He puts his finger to his lips. `Sssh. The Unspoken One.'

Visit the temple of the Three Fortunes	turn to **146**
Visit to shrine of Alvir and Valmir	turn to **503**
Visit Glimbinki's shrine	turn to **259**
Look for Badogor's fane	turn to **333**
Consider your other options	turn to **44**

129

Green sea flashes under trails of frothy white; looking north, you have the coast in sight.

The mate's gaze is fixed, not on land, but on the deep swelling waves. `How many skulls gaze up from the ocean bed?' he wonders. `How many sunken hulks, weed-choked and silent, lie rotting on the wet sands? Ah, it's always when we're nearly home that my fancies turn morbid.'

Roll two dice.

Score 2-6 The High King's banner	turn to **381**
Score 7-11 Plain sailing	turn to **475**
Score 12 An uncanny awakening	turn to **273**

130

You sit down and start drinking with them. Your aim is to lull their suspicions until they are soundly drunk and then make a reckoning for their crime.

To succeed, you must make a CHARISMA roll at a Difficulty of 11; failure means they take offence.

Successful CHARISMA roll	turn to **148**
Failed CHARISMA roll	turn to **73**

131

You order your men below and tell them to secure the hatches, knowing that the mermaids' singing will otherwise draw them to their doom.

`But what about the wheel, skipper?' asks the helmsman. `If I leave it untended who knows where we'll end up?'

He has a point. If you have a length of **rope** you could lash yourself to the wheel. Otherwise you'll have to go below with the others or stay on deck and take your chances.

Tie yourself to the wheel	turn to **353**
Go below with the crew	turn to **439**
Remain on deck	turn to **149**

132

It is with mounting excitement that you recognize this island as the one marked on the map.

Digging at the spot marked, you find a chest containing a handsome haul.

Roll one die to see what it is.

Score 1   100 Shards and a **sword (COMBAT +3)**
Score 2   400 Shards and a **compass (SCOUTING +1)**
Score 3   200 Shards and **plate armour (Defence +5)**
Score 4   300 Shards and an **ebony wand (MAGIC +2)**
Score 5   1000 Shards and a **candle**
Score 6   300 Shards and a **pirate captain's head**

When you have recorded the details of your treasure on your Adventure Sheet, cross off the **treasure map** and turn to **150**.

133

You find a half-buried chest under a stand of trees at the back of a beach of ash-grey sand. Inside is treasure worth 450 Shards and a **heart-shaped locket**.

Just as you are about to open the locket, you hear a voice calling you and look up to see a beautiful girl wearing garlands of flowers. She reaches down from the rock on which she's standing and asks you to return the locket to her.

Give it to her	turn to **76**
Refuse	turn to **95**

134

If you have a ship docked at Smogmaw you can either put to sea or sail upriver. Alternatively you may be able to hire passage aboard a merchant ship. In either case you will need to go to the quayside. It is also possible to travel on from here on foot, of course, but you are warned that the hinterland consists of wild jungle and dangerous marshes.

Go to the quayside	turn to **71**
Travel overland	turn to **90**
Remain in Smogmaw	turn to **44**

135

Your current position is south of the Sleeping Isle. The bottom edges of your charts show a fancifully-drawn morass of swampland and rank jungle – the unexplored continent of Ankon-Konu.

Go west	turn to **79**
Go east	turn to **153**
Go north	turn to **468**
Go south	*The Lone and Level Sands* **200**

136

The ocean stretches as far as the eye can see. It is tranquil, but there is something ominous about the silence. Roll two dice.

Score 2-4	A hurricane	turn to **139**
Score 5-8	A quiet voyage	turn to **154**
Score 9-12	Treachery aboard!	turn to **292**

137

You are at sea south of Sokara, at a point roughly on the same longitude as Trefoille. You consider your next course.

South	turn to **4**
North	turn to **66**
East	turn to **246**
West	turn to **81**

138

Drifting in a light fog, you are startled by the sound of ripping canvas and splintering wood. The ship lurches to a dead halt, then begins to turn about. The cause is almost unbelievable: an anchor, dangling from above the fog bank, has lodged against the forecastle! As you watch, a spindly fellow with violet skin comes scrambling down and tries to work the anchor free.

| Order the violet man seized | turn to **251** |
| Let him do his work and depart | turn to **228** |

139

The sky turns sulphur-grey. Thunderheads pile up on the horizon like vengeful gods. Lightning flickers like burning pitch on the world's rim. 'It's the end!' shrieks the bosun. 'Say your prayers, lads!'

If you have the blessing of Alvir and Valmir, which confers Safety from Storms, you can ignore the storm. Cross off your blessing and

turn to **154**.

Without a blessing to save you, the hurricane strikes. Roll one die if your ship is a barque, two dice if it is a brigantine, or three dice if a galleon. Add 1 to the roll if you have an excellent crew; subtract 1 if you have a poor crew.

Score 0-5	Your ship sinks	turn to **157**
Score 6-7	The mast splits	turn to **581**
Score 8-19	You weather the storm	turn to **98**

140

Whether you beg for mercy or vow vengeance, it is all the same to these merciless reavers. You are thrown into the sea. Make a SCOUTING roll at a Difficulty of 15.

Successful SCOUTING roll	turn to **158**
Failed SCOUTING roll	turn to **123**

141

You hold out your hand and begin to chant prayers of great power. 'That's it, skipper,' says the first mate encouragingly, 'give the wight a bit of holy hellfire!'

Make a SANCTITY roll at a Difficulty of 15.

Successful SANCTITY roll	turn to **195**
Failed SANCTITY roll	turn to **85**

142

This will be a test of your ingenuity, leadership and survival skills. Roll one die (two dice if you are a Wayfarer) and add your Rank.

Score 2-7	Overcome by thirst	turn to **123**
Score 8+	You reach Dweomer	turn to **152**

143 ☐

If the box above is empty, put a tick in it now and turn to **179**. If it was already ticked, turn to **161**.

144

A new dawn brings another chance of rescue. Roll two dice.

Score 2-9	An empty horizon	turn to **177**

Score 10   A merchantman   turn to **198**
Score 11-12   Pirates   turn to **218**

145

Should you try to slow your crew's breathing so that they can survive longer, or go for broke and try cancelling out the waterspout altogether? You must rely on your experience in such matters to guide you.

Make a MAGIC roll at a Difficulty of 14.
Successful MAGIC roll   turn to **163**
Failed MAGIC roll   turn to **181**

146

The temple of the Three Fortunes is an oval house with a triple-peaked thatched roof. The priestess is a young woman who is lounging on a jewelled divan, being fanned by two slave boys.
If an initiate   turn to **256**
If not an initiate   turn to **274**

147

You swim out to the shrine of the sea gods. Roll one die.
Score 1   A crocodile snaps at you, lose 1-6 Stamina
Score 2   You lose your purse, cross off all your cash
Score 3-6   You reach the shrine without incident

Assuming you survive, you touch the obelisk and receive a blessing of Safety from Storms, as long as you didn't have one already. Note this in the Blessings box on your Adventure Sheet.

To swim back you must make another SCOUTING roll at Difficulty 11.
Successful SCOUTING roll   turn to **44**
Failed SCOUTING roll   turn to **165**

148

Eventually they are sleeping like babes – like babes who have put away three bottles of the local firewater, that is. You carry them to the quayside and sell them to a slaver out of Port Kunrir. The total profit for the evening comes to a thoroughly satisfying 407 Shards.

Lose the codeword *Church* and turn to **44**.

149

All who hear the mermaids' song are drawn to their doom. Your one hope lies in the possibility that you are tone deaf. There is no chance of this if you are a Troubadour; for any other profession, roll two dice and on a score of 2 you are tone deaf.

If you turn out to be tone deaf, turn to **300**. If not, get the codeword *Cerumen* before turning to **333** in *Into the Underworld*.

150

There is not much food to be had on the island, but your crew gather some shellfish and someone succeeds in bringing down a seagull with a slingshot. That night you dine on your first fresh stew in weeks. Recover 1-6 Stamina points if injured and then turn to **278**.

151

You have been washed up in a small harbour. Many fishing boats painted in gay colours lie on the tide-streaked mud. A pretty town of whitewashed cottages stretches steeply up from the quayside towards high cliffs.

You climb the harbour steps and explore the streets. You soon discover that the place is under a curse, as all the villagers stand frozen like statues.

Take a boat to sea	turn to **411**
Ascend the cliffs	turn to **540**
Pray for guidance	turn to **467**
Rest in one of the houses	turn to **524**
Leave the town	turn to **449**

152

Note on your Ship's Manifest that your ship is docked at Dweomer harbour.

Turn to **100**.

153

By day you sail on lavender waves under a vault of azure and gold. By night the sails gleam dazzlingly white in the rays of the moon, and each star finds its twin in the dark ocean depths.

Recover 1 Stamina point if injured, then roll two dice.

Score 2-5	A flock of birds	turn to **239**
Score 6	An uneventful journey	turn to **171**
Score 7-12	Landfall	turn to **57**

154

You are crossing the Sea of Hydras, a stretch of water with a baleful reputation. The crewmen go about their tasks in uneasy silence, hardly daring to draw breath lest they attract the attention of calamitous misfortune.

Go south	turn to **23**
Go north east	*Lords of the Rising Sun* **202**
Go north	*Lords of the Rising Sun* **309**
Go south east	turn to **98**
Go west	turn to **337**

155

Despite the overcast sky, you think you have a good estimate of your position.

'We are due south of Yellowport,' you tell the navigator, who looks back at you dubiously. 'Set your bearing accordingly.'

Go north	*The War-Torn Kingdom* **29**
Go south	turn to **246**
Go east	turn to **55**
Go west	turn to **77**

156

You approach the Island of Fire. It comprises a broad mountain of volcanic origin rimmed by fertile plains. Islanders wave to you from the water's edge.

| Put in at the island | turn to **461** |
| Continue on to open ocean | turn to **479** |

157

Helpless in the hurricane's grip, your vessel is torn apart. Water rushes into the broken shell of the hull, dragging you down. The screams of your crewmen are lost the roar of the storm. Cross off your ship and crew; they are lost. So are your money and possessions. You can think of nothing now but saving yourself.

Roll two dice. If the score is greater than your Rank, you are drowned (turn to **123**). If the score is less than or equal to your Rank, you manage to stay alive by clinging to a broken spar. On the point of death, with your vision blurring, you see a ship. Seawater fills your mouth as you try to cry out; all you manage is a feeble groan. The ship seems to jump closer in rapid flickering movements as you drift in and out of consciousness. At last you feel yourself being hauled aboard.

You wake on a pallet below deck. You start to sit up, but you are still too weak after your ordeal.

'Save your strength,' says a voice out of the gloom. 'You'll need it. The life of a slave is harsh indeed.'

You discover that you have been picked up by an Uttakin slave ship. The slavers will only agree to release you if you can pay a ransom of 300 Shards.

Pay the ransom	*Cities of Gold and Glory* **229**
Can't or won't pay	*The Court of Hidden Faces* **321**

158

Somehow you manage to keep your head above water. You swim until your limbs feel as though they are caught in a net. You struggle on, mortally weak but determined not to give up.

A ship heaves into view. You raise your arm and give a feeble cry. By some miracle you are spotted, and the ship steers towards you. You are hauled aboard, wrapped in blankets and given a bowl of hot soup.

To your immense relief, you have been rescued by merchants from Metriciens. 'We are bound for Dweomer and then home,' they say. 'We'll drop you off wherever you like.'

Get off at Dweomer	turn to **100**
Continue on to Metriciens	*Cities of Gold and Glory* **48**

159

The island is a tropical paradise. You decide to treat your crew to a week of rest and relaxation.

To see how it affects them, roll two dice and add your Rank.

Score 3-6   The crew maroons you. Turn to **177**

Score 7-9	Indiscipline: reduce Crew Quality by one step
Score 10-11	Invigoration: upgrade Crew Quality by one step
Score 12+	Inspiration: upgrade Crew Quality two steps

The four categories of Crew Quality are poor, average, good and excellent. Crew Quality cannot go below poor or above excellent.

When you are ready to set sail again (assuming you aren't marooned!) turn to **41**.

160

Get the codeword *Callid*.

All you can do is trust to luck. Roll two dice.

Score 2-6	Overcome by thirst	turn to **123**
Score 7-12	An island lies ahead	turn to **30**

161

Fiddler's Green is an isle of perfect peace and contentment, where brooks gurgle through delightful woodland and there are wide lawns where you can bask all day in the sun.

If you are injured, restore your Stamina to its normal (unwounded) score. Also, if your crew is of poor quality then the stay here upgrades them to average quality.

When you are ready to be on your way, turn to **125**.

162

You begin to suffer from stomach cramps followed by bouts of nausea. Perhaps it was those berries you picked? If you have a blessing of Immunity to Disease/Poison, you wake the next morning feeling fine (and remember to cross off the blessing). Otherwise you lose 1-6 Stamina points.

If still alive, turn to **144**.

163

There's no way you can cancel the waterspout with a spell – not in time to save the crew, anyway. You put them into a deep slumber to buy time, then consider your next course.

Dive into the sea	turn to **199**
Climb down the side of the ship	turn to **219**

164

Sailing away from the Unnumbered Isles after divers adventures.

Steer westwards	turn to **504**
Steer north towards the mainland	turn to **402**
Steer south for Ankon-Konu	turn to **42**
Steer east	turn to **81**

165

You are swept away by the current and eventually carried back to the bank. By this time you are bruised and weary and you have got several mouthfuls of foul muddy water.

Lose 2 Stamina points. Also, unless you have a blessing of Immunity to Disease/Poison, you become sick with malaria and must permanently lose 1 from all your attributes except SANCTITY. (Remember to cross off the blessing if you had one.)

Turn to **44**.

166

You seek to shame them by pointing out their shortcomings in comparison with the great and noble deeds of the gods. This requires you to make a SANCTITY roll at a Difficulty of 15; failure means that you only manage to arouse them to ire.

Successful SANCTITY roll	turn to **184**
Failed SANCTITY roll	turn to **73**

167

If you just sold a **pirate captain's head**, turn to **185**. If not, turn to **44**.

168

Lightning unfolds like vast snapping banners across a sky filled with wind-tossed clouds. If you have a blessing of Safety from Storms, cross it off and turn to **352**.

Otherwise splinters of lightning fall from the sky and leap along the spars. Roll two dice; add 1 to the roll if you possess a lump of **copper ore**.

Score 2-4	The mainmast topples	turn to **212**
Score 5-10	Several sailors lost; reduce Crew Quality to poor	turn to **135**
Score 11+	Struck by lightning	turn to **123**

169

You put in at the island where you are regarded as a great hero. Seeing your return, fishermen turn their boats back to the quay and call their wives and children to prepare a feast in your honour.

Go to the market	turn to **318**
Talk to the wise woman	turn to **390**
Rest at home	turn to **335**
Upgrade your crew	turn to **349**
Set sail	turn to **298**

170

'Ah, this is the life!' you hear the cabin boy telling himself. 'One day I'll be as rich as the captain, and then I'll buy my own ship.'

You put a hand on his shoulder, startling him out of his reverie. 'In the meantime, lad, you'd better see to your chores,' you growl at him. 'Else we'll hear the ship's cat purring before the day is done.'

You sail on. Roll two dice.

Score 2-5	A magical wind	turn to **237**
Score 6-8	An uneventful journey	turn to **188**
Score 9-12	Murder most foul	turn to **659**

171

You estimate your position to be a little way north of the estuary of the Great River that cleaves across Ankon-Konu, separating the western desert and mountains from the thick foetid jungles of the east.

'What course, captain?' asks the mate.

North	turn to **244**
South	*The Lone and Level Sands* **300**
East	turn to **189**
West	turn to **468**

172

Three things take no notice of men's lives: Fate, the weather and the tides. Against Fate and storms, man may contend; but the sea's ferocity only Heaven can forfend.

Roll two dice.

Score 2-6	Lost cargo	turn to **629**
Score 7-9	An uneventful passage	turn to **190**
Score 10-12	Yellow plague	turn to **611**

173

A windy day with white clouds flying, flung spray and blown spume and the seagulls wheeling overhead – what more could a ship's captain ask for?

Recover 1 Stamina point if injured, then roll two dice.

Score 2-8	A quiet voyage	turn to **191**
Score 9-12	Trouble aboard	turn to **325**

174

Huge guns boom in the black battlefield that the sky has become. The sailors go white with fear. 'It's no mere storm,' screeches the bosun. 'It's the final battle of the gods! It's Armageddon!'

If you have the blessing of Alvir and Valmir, which confers Safety from Storms, you can ignore the storm. Cross off your blessing and turn to **209**.

Otherwise the storm hits with titanic fury, ripping huge waves out of the sea and flinging them across the deck. Roll one die if your ship is a barque, two dice if it is a brigantine, or three dice if a galleon. Add 1 to the roll if you have an excellent crew; subtract 1 if you have a poor crew.

Score 0-4	Your ship sinks	turn to **212**
Score 5-6	The mast splits	turn to **670**
Score 7-19	You weather the storm	turn to **227**

175

The avenue between Dweomer and the harbour is a metalled road lined with fanciful statues. Looking inland, you can see the gleam of blue light emanating from a dense wood.

Head towards the wood turn to **697**	
Go into the city	turn to **571**
Go to the harbour	turn to **100**

176

You emerge from your cabin to find all hands on deck and the ship speeding ahead under a full press of sail. It is with some astonishment that you see another vessel far astern.

'They're pirates, skipper,' says the mate. 'Been on our tail since the end of the last watch, but I think we can outrun them.'

'I should have been woken up at once!' you tell him severely.

Continue to run from the pirates	turn to **194**
Drop sail and turn to face them	turn to **214**

177

The island appears to have sufficient food and fresh water to sustain you, but it will not be like living in the lap of luxury.

Try to survive off the land	turn to **88**
Set to work building a raft	turn to **108**
Pray for deliverance	turn to **126**

178

The tunnel winds in a spiral towards the centre of the black island.

'It must be a fort,' says one of your crewmen.

'Not built by human hand,' says another, pointing to strange lines etched into the walls. They seem to show squat crab-men with many stalk-like eyes striding belligerently across the decks of ships, but it is hard to be sure in the dim light.

A black stone door with an opal panel in the middle blocks the way ahead. To open it you will need a **sea-green lens**.

Open the door	turn to **216**
Return the way you came	turn to **196**

179

With your own eyes you have seen Fiddler's Green – a myth spoken of by every seaman.

If you are Mage, Troubadour or Wayfarer, this unique experience gives you the chance to go up in Rank. Roll two dice. You gain a Rank if the score on the dice is above your current Rank. This means you gain 1-6 Stamina points permanently: increase your normal (unwounded) Stamina score by the roll of one die. Remember that going up a Rank also increases your Defence.

Priests, Warriors and Rogues get no chance to increase in Rank; the beauty of Fiddler's' Green leaves them unmoved.

Once you have made the necessary adjustments to your Adventure Sheet, turn to **161**.

180

The raft finally breaks apart, but not before it has carried you to a stretch of shoreline. You have no idea where you might be, but at least you have reached the mainland. Or have you?

Roll one die.

Score 1-2	turn to **26**
Score 3	turn to **505**
Score 4-5	turn to **238**
Score 6	turn to **313**

181

You waste precious minutes fumbling with a spell that is far beyond your ability. Meanwhile, the crew choke silently to death in the rarefied atmosphere. Realizing there is nothing you can do here, you lower yourself from the side and drop down into the sea. Turn to **199**.

182

On the south of the island you find a sheltered bay surrounded by high mist-cloaked crags.

'This would make a good anchorage, skipper,' says the first mate.

Drop anchor here	turn to **220**
Continue around the island to Dweomer	turn to **152**
Sail away from the island	turn to **122**

183 ☐

The vessel is listing badly and not worth salvaging, but you send a party across to see if she has any cargo. If the box above is empty, put a tick in it and turn to **202**. If the box was already ticked, turn to **221**.

184

They begin to weep bitterly and repent their crime. You are so moved by their renewed pledges of loyalty that you forgive them for stranding you on the island.

If you have a ship docked at Smogmaw, the three mutineers join the crew. They are seasoned seamen, so this increases the crew quality by one step (from poor to average, average to good, or good to excellent).

Lose the codeword *Church* and turn to **314**.

185

Half the inhabitants of Smogmaw are pirates or the friends of pirates. No doubt the trophy you just sold was recognized by someone, because as you are walking past a row of shanties you are struck in the neck by a poisoned dart.

If you have a blessing of Immunity to Disease/Poison, cross it off and turn to **44**. Otherwise you can do nothing to save yourself; turn to **123**.

186

The catamarans are packed with raiders from the coast of Ankon-Konu. They cannot hope to take your ship, but they will try to leap aboard and carry off a few prisoners.

Roll two dice (three if you are a Warrior) and add your Rank to the number rolled.

Score 2-3	An arrow impales your eye	turn to **123**
Score 4-12	The raiders retreat at last	turn to **206**
Score 13+	You drive them off with ease	turn to **352**

187

If you have the codeword *Cacogast*, turn to **225**.

Otherwise the irascible college cook bars your way. 'I don't want any scholars in my kitchen!' he thunders.

To pacify him you could offer a **smoulder fish** (if you have one) or else rely on your natural charm, in the form of a CHARISMA roll at Difficulty 12.

Offer a **smoulder fish**	turn to **243**
Successful CHARISMA roll	turn to **261**
Failed CHARISMA roll	turn to **279**

188

You study the charts, reckoning your position to lie due south of the estuary of the Ruby River. Far to the east on this latitude lies the Island of Fire.

Steer south	turn to **370**
Go west	turn to **96**
Head north	turn to **21**
Travel east	turn to **208**

189

A strong tropical wind strains the sails. 'Best we strike the topsail,' says the mate. 'If a storm hits we're in danger of capsizing.'

Roll two dice.

Score 2-4	Storm	turn to **174**
Score 5-8	Nothing of note	turn to **209**
Score 9-12	Madness	turn to **106**

190

Ringed about with desolate shores, the sea keeps up its eternal whisperings. It puts the mate, who is normally an irascible red-faced drunkard, in wistful mood. 'Often when at home,' he says, 'tiring of laughter and song, I take myself to a deserted bay and listen for the sea-nymphs' flutes that herald the tide.'

'You're a poet!' says the navigator admiringly.

The mate glares at him, jerked back to his usual foul mood. 'There's no call for insults, mister! Look alive – we need a new course, you swab.'

Go east	*Lords of the Rising Sun* **309**
Go west	turn to **156**
Go north	turn to **173**
Go south	turn to **337**

191

Out of a grey dawn, the tall peaks of an island show like a blood-rimmed saw against the sky. It is Dragon Island.

Go east to the island	*Lords of the Rising Sun* **90**
Go west	turn to **210**
Go north	turn to **55**
Strike south for open seas	turn to **172**

192

Starspike Island is a breathtaking sight: from its centre a slender mountain rises straight up into the sky. Its pinnacle is lost far beyond the clouds. 'It's said to be higher than Sky Mountain in Sokara,' says one of your crewmen.

<table>
<tr><td>Put in at the island</td><td>turn to 704</td></tr>
<tr><td>Sail off</td><td>turn to 230</td></tr>
</table>

193

The daylight is suddenly blotted out by vast clouds that spread like pools of ink across the sky. Lightning forms an incessant web from horizon to horizon, and the thunder is like being inside a great bronze bell. You bellow orders, but they are lost on the wind. The crew stare all around, limp with fear. Only luck can save you now.

If you have the blessing of Alvir and Valmir, which confers Safety from Storms, you can ignore the storm. Cross off your blessing and turn to **61**.

If you have no blessing, the storm hits with full force. Rain rattles against the juddering canvas; waves lash the deck. Roll one die if your ship is a barque, two dice if it is a brigantine, or three dice if a galleon. Add 1 to the roll if you have an excellent crew; subtract 1 if you have a poor crew.

Score 0-4	Your ship sinks	turn to **249**
Score 5-6	The mast splits	turn to **670**
Score 7-19	You weather the storm	turn to **81**

194

Roll two dice and add your Rank. Add 1 to the total if you have an average crew, 2 if you have a good crew, or 3 if you have an excellent crew.

Score 1-5	The pirates overtake you	turn to **214**
Score 6+	You outrun them	turn to **61**

195

The creature throws up its bloodless hands, utters a terrible howl, and vanishes like smoke on the wind. The echoes of its final cry are a long time in dying away.

'Whew!' says the bosun in a trembling voice. 'Good job we got it before moonrise, or its strength would've doubled.'

Explore its lair	turn to **215**
Sail away right now	turn to **41**

196

You return to the ship and sail away. Cross off a **candle** if you used one. Then, if you have the codeword *Callid*, lose it and turn to **717**. Otherwise, turn to **48**.

197

Your master at arms leaps at the stranger, only to end up flat on his back across the deck. The carpenter, a burly tavern brawler, fares no better.

'Do you send your minions to fight me, then?' roars the stranger. 'I expected better of a ship's captain!'

Fight him yourself	turn to **235**
Tell him to calm down	turn to **217**

198

You are picked up by merchants from Yellowport who come ashore to replenish their supplies. They are amazed to find a human being living here.

'We are bound for Imperial Chambara, then hope to do some trading in the south,' they say. 'Would you like to be dropped off anywhere, or will you stay aboard till we get home?'

Disembark at Chambara	*Lords of the Rising Sun* **79**
Ask to be dropped off at Smogmaw	turn to **44**
Continue on to Yellowport	*The War-Torn Kingdom* **140**

199

You strike the water with enough force to knock the wind out of you. Lose 1-3 Stamina points (the score of one die halved, rounding fractions up). If you survive, the current steadily carries you away from the waterspout atop which your old ship will float forever in the clouds. Delete the ship and crew from your Adventure Sheet; also cross off your money and possessions.

You drift for hours until picked up by a warship out of Port Kunrir. 'We'll drop you off at the Faceless King's court,' says the captain.

'Good. I can arrange passage home from there.'

He laughs. 'I doubt it! Slaves aren't allowed quite that degree of freedom.'

Turn to **321** in *The Court of Hidden Faces*.

200

`We're making better headway now,' announces the mate. `Let's just hope that we don't run afoul of the weather.' Roll two dice.

Score 2-3	Pirates	turn to **654**
Score 4-5	Storm	turn to **544**
Score 6-8	An uneventful voyage	turn to **311**
Score 9-12	Lights under the waves	turn to **711**

201

By dawn you have managed to overhaul two of the pirate ships, but the first presses on relentlessly, steadily gaining on your less manoeuvrable vessel. Pulling alongside, they cast grappling hooks and come swarming aboard.

Roll three dice if you are a Warrior, or two dice if you belong to any other profession. Add your Rank to this roll. Then, if your crew is poor quality, subtract 2 from the total. If the crew is good quality, add 2. If the crew is excellent quality, add 3.

Score 0-3	Calamity; you are killed	turn to **123**
Score 4-8	Crushing defeat; lose 2-12 Stamina	turn to **435**
Score 9-12	Forced to give in; lose 1-6 Stamina	turn to **416**
Score 13-16	The pirates withdraw	turn to **101**
Score 17+	Outright victory	turn to **307**

202

The captain's log contains some interesting accounts of his travels across the Great Steppes. You are particularly interested in a detailed description of a tomb he found. `It is only possible to gain entrance when the gods are not looking,' the captain has written in his log. `We were unable to penetrate to the heart of the tomb, but returned to the ship with much booty from the outer chambers.'

Get the codeword *Cheops* and turn to **221**.

203

The three mutineers leave after a while, each clutching a bottle of strong spirit. You follow them through the maze of boardwalks and low-eaved shacks.

Make a SCOUTING roll at a Difficulty of 14; failure means that you lose them.

Successful SCOUTING roll	turn to **222**
Failed SCOUTING roll	turn to **44**

204

By night you dream of a frightful fiend with flesh the colour of cold clay, only to wake with a shiver and find it was no dream. The fiend holds aside the curtain of your bunk in one taloned hand, leaning forward with black mouth agape. You can smell its seaweed breath; its eyes are like dull pearls in the candlelight.

If you have the codeword *Cull*, turn to **223**. Otherwise, turn to **241**.

205

You are entering the waters around the Unnumbered Isles. Somewhere in this reef-strewn archipelago is the stronghold of the Reavers. They rule like barbarian lords over the poor crofters of the isles.

If you have the codeword *Chance*, turn to **545**. If not, turn to **563**.

206

As the raiders leap back to their catamarans and veer away, it is left to you to count the cost of victory. You have lost 2-12 Stamina points (the roll of two dice) in the fighting. If you can survive that, roll one die.

Score 1-2	The raiders left empty-handed	turn to **352**
Score 3-4	They took all your fresh water	turn to **124**
Score 5-6	The crew blames your poor leadership	turn to **599**

207

The Master's lodgings are in a fine, old, stone house at the back of a lawn just inside the college gates. His lugubrious butler Mantel admits you into a study that smells of old books, pipe smoke and armchair leather.

'Who's this?' demands the Master, looking up from his chair.

'One of the students, I'm afraid, sir,' says Mantel.

Make a CHARISMA roll at a Difficulty of 14.

Successful CHARISMA roll   turn to **560**
Failed CHARISMA roll   turn to **578**

208

'See that blue glow along the horizon?' says the navigator. 'It's the witchlight that flickers over Braelak Isle.'

Roll two dice.

Score 2-5   A tempest   turn to **422**
Score 6-12   Nothing of note   turn to **226**

209

'Land ahoy!' shouts the lookout from the crow's nest.

'That's strange,' says the navigator, consulting his charts. 'There's no island marked.'

Investigate the island	turn to **30**
Sail on	turn to **48**

210

The deep and dark blue ocean rolls on around your bows, churned by a freshening wind. Roll two dice.

Score 2-4	A flying ship	turn to **138**
Score 5-8	Nothing	turn to **228**
Score 9-12	An exotic vessel	turn to **619**

211

The serpent raises its heavy head and gives vent to a sibilant snarl. Acid drips from its fangs as it snaps at you.

Serpent, COMBAT 7, Defence 8, Stamina 10

Lying in the shade has left it quite torpid, so you could easily run off rather than fight it.

Run back to the ship	turn to **125**
Kill the creature	turn to **12**

212

The ship cracks open and seawater rushes into the broken shell of the hull. The screams of your crewmen are drowned out by the surge of the waves. Cross off your ship and crew; they are lost. You can think of nothing now but saving yourself.

Roll two dice. If the score is greater than your Rank, you are drowned. If the score is less than or equal to your Rank, you are swept miraculously towards a beach of white sand fringed with feathery palms. Lose 2-12 Stamina points and (if you can survive that) turn to **559** in *The Serpent King's Domain*.

213

The sky turns black and spits lightning. Your crew grow fearful. 'Lay her a-hold!' cries the bosun in panic. 'Bestir yourselves, lads, or we're done for!'

If you have the blessing of Alvir and Valmir, which confers Safety from Storms, you can ignore the storm. Cross off your blessing and turn to **155**.

Otherwise the storm hits with titanic fury, throwing vast fists of water up from the sea to batter your ship's frail timbers. Roll one die if your ship is a barque, two dice if it is a brigantine, or three dice if a galleon. Add 1 to the roll if you have an excellent crew; subtract 1 if you have a poor crew.

Score 0-4	Your ship sinks	turn to **249**
Score 5-6	The mast splits	turn to **231**
Score 7-19	You weather the storm	turn to **246**

214

You close with the pirate vessel. At close quarters you see the attackers waiting with drawn swords at the rail. They are an odd mix of tall Uttakin, velvet-coated Golnirans, Sokarans with broad pale faces and savage natives of the Feathered Lands. All are alike in one respect, however: the naked hate that shines from their eyes. As the ships come together, they leap aboard with a wild battle-cry.

Roll two dice (three dice if you're a Warrior) and add your Rank. Then, if your crew is poor quality, subtract 2 from the total. If the crew is good, add 2. If the crew is excellent, add 3.

Score 0-3	Calamity; you are killed	turn to **123**
Score 4-8	Crushing defeat; lose 2-12 Stamina	turn to **140**
Score 9-12	Forced to give in; lose 1-6 Stamina	turn to **250**
Score 13-16	The pirates withdraw	turn to **245**
Score 17+	Outright victory	turn to **232**

215

Inside the cave is a stone sarcophagus that smells of brimstone and ammonia. Strewn around it, spotted with bat droppings and gobbets of rancid gristle, are piles of gold plate, coin and jewellery. Rubies sparkle like drops of black blood in the rays of the rising moon. Emeralds gleam like myriad cats' eyes. Sapphires are strewn about like crystalline petals.

The total value of the haul is 6000 Shards. Add this to your petty cash and turn to **41**.

216 ☐

You present the **sea-green lens** to the door panel and it slides up. Beyond is a circular courtyard open to the sky with a marble fountain in the middle.

'Blow me if we aren't smack in the bloomin' middle of the place!' says the master at arms.

If the box above is empty, put a tick in it and turn to **270**. If it was already ticked, turn to **252**.

217

'Your talk of peace insults me!' rages the bare-chested stranger. His fist lashes out, giving you such a strong buffet in the face that your knees buckle and blackness drops over you like a great wave. By the time your crew can bring you round, the stranger has sailed off in his boat.

Lose 1 Stamina point permanently (that is, reduce your unwounded Stamina score by 1) and then turn to **125**.

218

Pirates find you when they come ashore to bury some treasure. Their captain fondles your hair and smirks.

'Young and healthy enough,' he says. 'You're bound for the slave pens, my friend, unless you can muster a ransom of 150 Shards.'

Agree to the ransom	*Cities of Gold and Glory* **229**
Can't or won't pay	turn to **472**

219

Dangling on a long rope usually used for keelhauling, you manage to get down to the top of the waterspout. From there you swim down to the sea bed, where you discover a rusty wheel beside a wide vent. Can this be the source of the waterspout?

With the last breath in your lungs, you turn the wheel until the vent closes and the torrent of water is cut off. Then you bob back to the surface to find your ship drifting safely on the waves once more. Your crew gratefully hauls you aboard with loud cheers.

`A strange experience,' you say to the first mate.

He waves his hand to make light of the matter. `Oh, a seafarer sees many strange things. Let me tell you about the time…'

And so you sail on. Turn to **39**.

220

Note that your ship is docked in the southern bay on Sorcerers' Isle. Then turn to **407**.

221

There is 1 Cargo Unit of spices in the ship's hold, which you can take aboard if you have room for it. (You can, of course, jettison existing cargo to make room for it if you wish.)

The first mate reports finding no sign of life aboard the ship. `Looks like she was abandoned all of a sudden, captain,' he says. `We found a couple of things you might want.'

He hands you a **mariner's ruttier** and a **smoulder fish**. Note these items down if you want to keep them, then turn to **118**.

222

The three of them live in a house that stands on short wooden posts above a tract of mud on the southern fringe of town. You watch them slump in the doorway, where the jutting porch of interleaved pandanus shields them from the sun. The air is filled with gnats and the stench of rotting river weeds.

If you have the codeword *Aid* or have a ship docked at Smogmaw then you can round up some friends to help you exact your revenge. Otherwise you must deal with the mutineers yourself.

Muster some friends (if you have any)	turn to **240**
Attack the three on your own	turn to **73**
Wait till they're asleep	turn to **148**
Forget about them	turn to **44**

223

`You have not done as I asked,' whispers the fiend in a voice of dreadful intimacy.

You try to cry out, to call the men on watch to your aid. But the fiend touches your lips with an icy finger. 'Hush,' it says. 'No need to bother them with our business.'

With the other hand it reaches out and extinguishes the nightlight. Turn to **123**.

224

Remember to cross off the 35 Shards to pay for your berth.

The ship is the *Ichabod*, a barque with fading paintwork and weathered timbers. Three days out from Smogmaw she runs into heavy weather.

Roll one die.

Score 1-4	Arrive at Yellowport as planned; turn to *The War-Torn Kingdom* **10**
Score 5-6	The *Ichabod* is forced to lay up at Copper Island for repairs; turn to **99**

225

Woe betide any scholar to whom the cook has taken a dislike. You are fed a bowl of hot stew which you consume with gusto, but later that evening you suffer stomach pains and are up until dawn retching into a bucket.

Lose 1-6 Stamina points (the score of one die) and then turn to **607**.

226

You are roughly twenty leagues due north of the Sleeping Isle. The helmsman awaits your orders.

Go east	turn to **9**
Go west	turn to **170**
Go north	turn to **129**
Go south	turn to **281**

227

Closing your eyes, you lean back against the mast and enjoy the rise and plunge of the ship as she steers on through warm tropical seas.

Recover 1 Stamina point if injured. Then roll two dice.

Score 2-4	Storm	turn to **248**
Score 5-7	Nothing of note	turn to **245**

Score 8-9   A castaway   turn to **515**
Score 10-12   Pirates   turn to **176**

228

You are roughly midway between the Isle of Fire and Dragon Island.
What course will you tell your men to steer?

North   turn to **55**
South   turn to **172**
East   turn to **173**
West   turn to **246**

229

You give a faltering tongue-tied apology that softens the men's wrath
but leaves them openly contemptuous. The first mate, Fryer, takes
command and you are set ashore on a deserted island to fend for yourself.

Cross off your ship and her cargo. They are lost for ever. Your main
problem now is just staying alive.

Get the codeword *Church* and turn to **177**.

230

You set a new course, and eventually even the lofty pinnacle of
Starspike Island drops below the horizon.

Go north   turn to **156**
Go south   turn to **337**
Go east   turn to **172**
Go west   turn to **302**

231

The ship is swept far out to sea. Men and goods are washed overboard
by huge waves that snap your hawsers like twine. Lose 1 Cargo Unit (if
you have any cargo) and reduce your crew quality by one step – i.e. an
excellent crew becomes good, a good crew becomes average, and an
average crew becomes poor. (A poor crew can't get any worse!)

At last the storm blows itself out. You are left drifting in unknown
waters.

Turn to **321**.

232

You help yourself to the pirates' treasure, which amounts to 250 Shards. Record it on your Adventure Sheet.

Their ship's hold contains 2 Cargo Units of spices, which you can add to your own cargo if your ship has enough room for them.

Once you have made the necessary adjustments to your Adventure Sheet, turn to **245**.

233

You are face to face with Amcha One-Eye, the bane of honest merchants throughout the northern lands. If you imagined that he would wear an eye-patch you were mistaken. His sightless eye is kept openly displayed, an unblinking white orb that strikes terror into the hearts of all who must confront him.

If you possess a **pirate captain's head**, turn to **493**.

If not, turn to **400**.

234

A figure composed of glittering green light appears in the air in front of
you. Your crewmen fall on their faces in abject fear. You are not so
easily cowed, but none the less you make a respectful bow.

'I recognize you as a worshipper of the Lord and Lady of the Sea,'
says the spectral figure. 'One boon shall I grant you. Choose whether
it is life, strength or ease that is your heart's desire.'

Choose life	turn to **289**
Choose strength	turn to **309**
Choose ease	turn to **327**

235

'Good!' he bellows. 'Good! Yes, by the two gods who rule below – I'll
grapple with you.'

He stamps the deck with such exuberant ferocity that even the
bravest of your men go scurrying for cover.

Make a COMBAT roll at a Difficulty of 13.

Successful COMBAT roll	turn to **271**
Failed COMBAT roll	turn to **253**

236

Witches come bouncing out across the waves, demonstrating their
contempt of nature's laws by riding in worm-eaten coracles that are as
leaky as sieves.

'Blow winds and crack your cheeks!' they cry, adding an obscene
laugh that causes disgust and horror in equal doses.

'They'll curse us to the ocean deeps,' moans the bosun in abject fear.
'Do something, captain!'

Make a MAGIC roll at a Difficulty of 15.

Successful MAGIC roll	turn to **254**
Failed MAGIC roll	turn to **272**

237

A wind of frightening intensity blows up out of nowhere. 'This weather
cannot be natural!' says the bosun with a shiver.

You round on him. 'You always say that, mister. Where's your
evidence?'

He points all around. 'The sheets of green lightning beyond the clouds. That thick sulphurous dust in the air. The presence of frogs and other unexplained debris in the water all around us.'

You give a snort. 'Fair enough.'

To cancel the supernatural wind you must make a MAGIC roll at a Difficulty of 15.

Successful MAGIC roll	turn to **188**
Failed MAGIC roll	turn to **255**

238

You are washed up on a narrow stretch of beach at the back of a bay surrounded by high mist-shrouded peaks. After resting to recover your strength, you pick your way up a series of steep paths until you can get a clear view of the island. To the north lies an expanse of glittering blue forest, so there can be no question where you are – Braelak, the Sorcerers' Isle. Nearer at hand is a tower built of obsidian blocks.

Enter the forest	turn to **697**
Go to the tower	turn to **426**

239

A flock of migrating birds alights to cover every inch of deck, masts and spars. Their plumage is a striking mixture of ebony, scarlet, and metallic green.

'Queer sort of birds,' remarks the mate. 'Got almost a wise look to them, wouldn't you say?'

Roll two dice.

Score 2	turn to **257**
Score 3-12	turn to **275**

240

With the help of a few strong men you have no trouble settling your score with the three mutineers. It is up to your own conscience what you do with them, but you can rest assured that you will never see them again.

Lose the codeword *Church* and turn to **44**.

241

'Pay heed to what I say,' whispers the fiend in gravid tones. 'Go north to a certain fane that is upon the Steppes, and there tell the four winds that Tayang Khan was foully slain at sea.'

You try twice to find your voice, finally managing to gasp out: 'What if they already know that?'

But the fiend seems not to understand. It speaks like a sleepwalker, repeating its words until they fade into incoherence. You watch it go as the candle burns down, and your rigid terror gradually gives way to fatigue. In the morning you are hardly sure it happened at all.

Get the codeword *Cull* and turn to **22**.

242

'Will we have any trouble reaching Dweomer?' you ask the skipper of the *Taradiddle*.

'Not in this beauty,' he says proudly. 'Her mast's of prime bluewood, and she always finds her way home.'

He is right; the voyage is blissfully uneventful. Remember to cross off the 35 Shards you had to pay for your passage, then turn to **100**.

243

The cook is delighted. This fish is rated a great delicacy by the dons of Dweomer. You are rewarded with 200 Shards. Cross the **smoulder fish** off your list of possessions and then turn to **607**.

244

'Can you taste it on the breeze, shipmates?' you ask the crew.

'Taste what, captain? The scent of brine?' asks the mate.

'No, not brine; it's the smell of sorcery. Braelak is just over the horizon.'

Roll two dice.

Score 2-4	A shooting star	turn to **460**
Score 5-7	A quiet day's sailing	turn to **262**
Score 8-12	Attacked by night	turn to **441**

245

With the navigator's spyglass you survey the tree-fringed cliffs and blazing coral beaches of Ankon-Konu. To the north across leagues of open ocean is Old Sokar, now renamed Marlock City since a coup in Sokara brought General Grieve Marlock to power.

Go north	turn to **42**
Go south	*The Serpent King's Domain* **200**
Go east	turn to **263**
Go west	turn to **189**

246

The days are fair and sunny, the nights star-brimmed. Your ship skims like a cloud across waves the colour of ink.

Recover 1 Stamina point if injured, then roll two dice.

Score 2-5	A vision in moonlight	turn to **665**
Score 6-8	A quiet day's sailing	turn to **264**
Score 9-12	Traders from Mithdrak	turn to **569**

247

You find a book that contains so many terrifying stories that you doubt if you'll ever sleep soundly again. It leaves you so scared that you have to wait for the librarian to come looking for you.

'Great tomes of fear!' he declares. 'Your hair has turned white.'

Lose 1 from CHARISMA and get the codeword *Chill*. Then turn to **368**.

248

The sky turns black and spits lightning. Your crewmen grow fearful.

'Lay her a-hold!' cries the bosun in panic. 'Bestir yourselves, lads, or we're done for!'

If you have the blessing of Alvir and Valmir, which confers Safety from Storms, you can ignore the storm. Cross off your blessing and turn to **245**.

Otherwise the storm hits with titanic fury, throwing vast fists of water up from the sea to batter your ship's frail timbers. Roll one die if your ship is a barque, two dice if it is a brigantine, or three dice if a galleon. Add 1 to the roll if you have an excellent crew; subtract 1 if you have a poor crew.

Score 0-4	Your ship sinks	turn to **212**
Score 5-6	The mast splits	turn to **670**
Score 7-19	You weather the storm	turn to **263**

249

The hull breaks into splinters and seawater gushes into the hold. Shuddering like a wounded beast, the ship begins to sink. The terrified cries of your crewmen are lost in the crash of the waves closing over your head. Cross off your ship and crew; they are lost. You can think of nothing now but saving yourself.

Roll two dice. If the score is greater than your Rank, you are drowned (turn to **123**). If the score is less than or equal to your Rank, you are swept miraculously towards a grim surf-lashed shore ringed with jagged reefs. Lose 2-12 Stamina points and (if you can survive that) turn to **313**.

250

The pirates take your cargo, all your possessions and your cash. They also seize your ship for themselves. Cross all these off your Adventure Sheet. At least they decide to spare your life – probably in the hope that you'll earn enough to buy another ship so they can rob you again.

You are put off in Smogmaw. Turn to **44**.

251

Several sailors grab the stranger and bring him over to you. You ply him with questions, but he has gone limp and begun to gasp for breath. He dies as quickly as a man might drown at six fathoms.

'What now, skipper?' says the first mate in an awestruck voice. 'Shall we cut the cable and let their ship go drifting off?'

| Cut the flying ship's cable | turn to **228** |
| Take a party of seamen aloft | turn to **269** |

252

Your crewmen take the opportunity to collect some barrels of fresh water from the fountain. Lose the codeword *Callid* if you had it.

There is nothing else of interest here, so you return to the ship. Turn to **196**.

253

The stranger grabs hold of you, hefts you into the air, and flings you down. You hit the deck with such force that it makes your teeth rattle. Lose 1-6 Stamina points (the score of one die) and decide whether you feel like fighting on.

Grapple your foe   turn to **235**
Tell him there's no need to fight   turn to **217**

254

You confound the witches by cancelling the spell that keeps their coracles afloat. Your crewmen laugh in relief as they watch the flotilla of vile women sink below the surging grey swell.

The leader of the coven manages to hold her head above water long enough to plead for you to haul her out.

Drop her a line	turn to **291**
Let her drown	turn to **39**

255

The wind does not abate for several hours. Somehow you have the uneasy feeling that it has blown you a quite unconscionable distance in that time.

After consulting the stars and his charts, the navigator makes a guess at your current position.

Roll two dice.

Score 2-3	turn to **228**
Score 4	turn to **320**
Score 5-6	turn to **118**
Score 7	turn to **648**
Score 8-9	turn to **322**
Score 10	turn to **283**
Score 11-12	turn to **352**

256

The priestess gets to her feet. 'The goddesses have looked on you with favour,' she says. 'Their breath has filled your sails, their hands sheltered your back, guiding you safely here.'

Seek a blessing from the goddesses	turn to **293**
Renounce their worship	turn to **330**
Leave the temple	turn to **44**

257

There are so many birds that, when they rise again into the air, their wings all but blot out the sun. At the same time you feel a strange enchantment creeping over you. But is it harmful, or beneficial? To resist the enchantment (assuming you want to try) you must succeed in a MAGIC roll at a Difficulty of 15.

| Resist the enchantment | turn to **171** |
| Fail to resist (or don't try) | turn to **294** |

258

If you have the codeword *Aid*, turn to **276**. If not, turn to **295**.

259

It is easy to pick out Glimbinki's shrine, a tall teepee of interlaced feathers supported by a central totem of hard red wood surmounted by a giant carved beak.

If you have the codeword *Cushat*, turn to **277**. If not, turn to **296**.

260

If you haven't already done so, cross off the 35 Shards that the captain wants to take you to Metriciens. Then roll one die.

| Score 1-2 | The captain is a villain. He takes all your money and maroons you; turn to **177** |
| Score 3-6 | You reach Metriciens without incident; turn to **48** in *Cities of Gold and Glory* |

261

The cook relents and lets you sit in a corner of the kitchen. The other scholars are impressed that you managed to charm even the bad-tempered cook, and your reputation soars. Roll one die. If the number rolled is higher than your CHARISMA score, increase it by 1. Now turn to **607**.

262

To the north lies Braelak, island of sorcerers. Far to the south are the marsh-enclosed ruins of old Tarshesh. Westwards there are the priests of Innis; pirates lurk in the east. Where now?

Head north	turn to **9**
Head south	turn to **153**
Head east	turn to **630**
Head west	turn to **281**

263

An offshore wind brings the scent of strange blossoms, dead vegetation and the stink of malarial swamps.

'The Weeping Jungle,' declares the mate gloomily. 'My brother lost his life in that pest-infested wilderness.'

The quartermaster expresses a sceptical view: 'I heard your brother died in a tavern brawl in Ringhorn.'

'Bah!' The mate stamps off to his cabin. You begin to worry about the crew's morale. Roll two dice.

Score 2-4	Mutiny!	turn to **612**
Score 5-8	A quiet voyage	turn to **282**
Score 9-10	Pirates	turn to **176**
Score 11-12	Divine intervention?	turn to **483**

264

Daybreak casts a net of mist across the water, blurring the horizon. It seems as though you are suspended in an infinite white void.

Steer north	turn to **66**
Go south	turn to **156**
Travel east	turn to **210**
Head west	turn to **119**

265

You can take the crewmen exploring with you or leave them here to gather supplies. If you decide to take the men, get the codeword *Cosy*.

You stroll through light woodland and emerge on a level plain. The grass is as neatly mown as a lawn. Bees hum drowsily between the flowers. A paved avenue, lined on either side by stone slabs, stretches off across the plain towards grey cliffs in the distance.

Go on	turn to **43**
Turn back	turn to **5**

266

Note that your ship is now docked at Smogmaw and then turn to **44**.

267

You help yourself to the pirates' treasure, which amounts to 400 Shards. Their ship's hold contains 1 Cargo Unit of spices, which you can add to your own cargo if your ship has room for it. Your mate is for taking the **pirate captain's head** as a gory trophy of your victory. Add it to your list of possessions if you agree.

You also get a chance to increase in Rank after your stirring leadership in battle. Roll two dice, and if the result is greater than your current Rank then you gain a Rank. You also gain 1-6 Stamina points permanently: increase your normal (unwounded) Stamina score by the roll of one die. Remember that going up a Rank increases your Defence.

Once you have made the necessary adjustments to your Adventure Sheet, turn to **101**.

268

The first mate comes running to your cabin in the small hours of the morning. 'Pirates, cap'n!' he gasps. 'Three ships coming in windward of us.'

You cannot battle three ships at once. You give orders to put out full sail. You must hope to outrun them.

Roll two dice and add your Rank. Add 1 to the total if you have an average crew, 2 if you have a good crew, or 3 if you have an excellent crew. Also, if your ship is carrying any Cargo Units, subtract 1 from the total.

Score 1-6	The pirates overtake you	turn to **201**
Score 7+	You shake them off	turn to **322**

269

Most are reluctant to go, but you find a pair of doughty fellows from Haggart's Corner who are too simple to understand fear. They follow you up into the rigging, from where you climb up the flying ship's anchor chain.

The deck is empty except for swirls of pearly mist. Glancing down, you can just make out the shadow of your own vessel under the blanket of fog. One of the seamen with you coughs and says, 'The air's perilous thin, skipper. Best shake a leg.'

Lose 1 Stamina point unless you have the codeword *Calcium*.

Go back down and be on your way   turn to **228**

Explore below decks   turn to **288**

270

A sacred aura hangs about this place. If you are an initiate of the twin gods of the sea, Alvir and Valmir, then you will be particularly attuned to it.

If you are an initiate of Alvir and Valmir, turn to **234**. Otherwise, turn to **252**.

271

You send him slamming to the deck, but he bounces up again none the worse for wear. Immediately he clasps his hand behind your neck and you are wrestling again.

Make a COMBAT roll at a Difficulty of 14.

Successful COMBAT roll   turn to **290**

Failed COMBAT roll   turn to **253**

272

The witches curse your crew with a dreary malaise that renders them useless for all but the simplest chores.

Reduce your crew's quality to poor. (If your crew is already of poor quality it can't get any worse and so the curse has no effect.)

Tittering evilly, the witches skim off across the choppy sea.

Turn to **39**.

273

You wake up. Something is amiss. It takes you a while to realize that you are no longer at sea. In fact, you are not even aboard a ship. Instead you are lying in a bed in one of the rooms at Chard's Inn.

How did you get here? It is a complete mystery. When you ask someone the date, you discover that six months are missing out of your life! Cross off your ship and crew – they are lost. Also lose the first 1-6 possessions written on your Adventure Sheet. Your money is gone too.

However, you have an additional point on your SCOUTING score that you picked up from somewhere, and if you were injured then your Stamina is now back to its normal score.

Get the codeword *Clutch* and turn to **120** in *Cities of Gold and Glory*.

274

The priestess holds up her hand before you can speak. 'Peace! Whatever your business, all must here adapt to a slower pace of life. Ah, this accursed heat.' She indicates her brow, and a slave boy runs forward to lick away the film of sweat.

You are faintly repelled by such decadence, but you try to hide it. 'I have come...' you begin.

The priestess frowns. 'Have I not said that things are done differently here in Smogmaw? Approach, sit; tell me your business over a game of cards.'

Agree to play with her	turn to **343**
Leave the temple	turn to **44**

275

Mysteriously, when the flock has departed you discover a stowaway squatting on the bowsprit. He peers at everyone suspiciously and utters cawing noises when approached, but after a few days he has recovered his wits enough to speak. 'I dreamt I was flying,' he says. 'Nor can I tell how I got here.'

He has some money saved up at home, and rewards you with 50 Shards for dropping him off at your next port of call.

Turn to **171**.

276

The merchant known as Moon of Evening will never forget how you saved her life. She takes you into her household and embellishes you with body paint and a **cloak of feathers** if you did not already have one. You can also stay here with her family for as long as you like – if injured, restore your Stamina to its normal unwounded score.

'Are you staying in Smogmaw?' asks Moon of Evening's brother, a handsome fellow known as Dances with Boas. 'I know a merchant who'll take you upriver if you like.'

Go with the merchant   *The Serpent King's Domain* **475**
Stay in town for now   turn to **295**

277

'You have performed a great service for Glimbinki,' avers the priest.
'In return I will bestow the two blessings that are within my power.'

Mark SCOUTING and MAGIC in the Blessings box on your Adventure
Sheet if they were not already written there. These blessings entitle you
to reroll a failed attempt at using the ability in question. Each blessing
can be used only once.

Thanking the priest, you return to town. Turn to **44**.

278

The island is soon left far astern.

Go north	*Lords of the Rising Sun* **202**
Go south	turn to **60**
Go east	*Lords of the Rising Sun* **102**
Go west	turn to **136**

279

The cook issues a stream of insults that threatens to turn the air blue. You retreat cowed and shaken. Lose 1 point of CHARISMA and acquire the codeword *Cacogast*, then turn to **607**.

280

The ghost disappears with a doleful sigh. A wisp of fabric drifts down to the deck. It is a **spectral veil**. Note it on your list of possessions if you decide to keep it, then turn to **78**.

281

The first mate breaks open a keg of beer and has all the crew raise their cups to the north. He excuses this by saying: 'We're toasting the High King. It's a time-honoured ritual, Cap'n.'

You smile indulgently. It has been three centuries since the Uttakin swept away the once-glorious realm of the High King, but old traditions die hard. Roll two dice.

Score 2-5 Songs across the waves	turn to **93**
Score 6-8 Nothing untoward	turn to **300**
Score 9-12 Uttakin slavers	turn to **450**

282

You are sailing in warm tropical waters the colour of ink.

If you have the codeword *Coracle*, turn to **341**. If you have the codeword *Certain*, turn to **87**. If you have the codeword *Covet*, turn to **107**. If you have none of those, turn to **125**.

283

You are sailing off the south-eastern promentary of Sokara, known for obscure reasons as Scorpion Bight. To the north lies the Druids' Isle.

Steer north   *The War-Torn Kingdom* **136**
Steer south   turn to **173**
Steer east   *Lords of the Rising Sun* **406**
Steer west   turn to **66**

284

While some of your crew see to repairs aboard ship, you lead a shore party in gathering food and fresh water.

Roll one die.

Score 1-2	You fall from a coconut palm; lose 1-6 Stamina
Score 3	Stung by a scorpion; lose 2-12 Stamina unless you have a blessing of Immunity to Disease/Poison
Score 4-6	You get a good rest; recover 1 Stamina if injured

When you are ready to leave the island, turn to **304**.

285

A sharp tang is on the air. The sky, thick with iron-coloured clouds, begins to spin slowly like a great inexorable wheel. The heavens are shot through with brimstone flares. The crew stands slack-faced with dismay. 'It is the fist of Elnir...' whimpers the bosun. 'He means to punish us for our sins.'

If you have the blessing of Alvir and Valmir, which confers Safety from Storms, you can ignore the storm. Cross off your blessing and turn to **320**.

If you have no such blessing, the hurricane sweeps down with merciless force. Roll one die if your ship is a barque, two dice if it is a brigantine, or three dice if a galleon. Add 1 to the roll if you have an excellent crew; subtract 1 if you have a poor crew.

Score 0-4	Your ship sinks	turn to **6**
Score 5-6	The mast splits	turn to **231**
Score 7+	You weather the storm	turn to **337**

286

The prow of the oncoming ship looms closer. Your men stand ready, braced for impact. It comes, the ship lurches, there is an instant's hesitation as though the Fates held their breath – then the pirates are aboard. Battle is joined.

Roll three dice if you are a Warrior, or two dice if you belong to any other profession. Add your Rank to this roll.

Then, if your crew is poor quality, subtract 2 from the total. If the crew is good quality, add 2. If the crew is excellent quality, add 3.

Score 0-4	Calamity; you are killed	turn to **123**
Score 5-9	Crushing defeat; lose 2-12 Stamina	turn to **435**
Score 10-13	Forced to give in; lose 1-6 Stamina	turn to **416**
Score 14-17	The pirates withdraw	turn to **101**
Score 18+	Outright victory	turn to **267**

287

Hardly able to contain your mirth at the thought of the great Reavers being robbed themselves, you help yourself to a few fistfuls of treasure (worth 500 Shards in all) before sneaking back out of their stronghold.

If you have the codeword *Crocus*, turn to **549**. Otherwise turn to **436**.

288

Lose 2 more Stamina points in the rarefied air if you don't have the codeword *Calcium*.

You descend a narrow gangway to a passage with a door to either side. You suspect that the two Golnir men with you are beginning to understand the difference between courage and recklessness.

Try the left-hand door	turn to **326**
Try the right-hand door	turn to **10**
Advance down the passage	turn to **29**
Return to your ship	turn to **308**

289

'Journey towards the rising sun,' says the herald of the twin gods. 'Before you reach the stars, you will come upon a bay that is guarded by a great serpent. Fight it alone – no man may help you. At the highest point of the island you'll get your boon.'

The figure dissolves in a cascade of fading green sparks.

Get the codeword *Coracle* and then turn to **252**.

290

Again you batter the strange fighter down. Now there is a thin smear of blood at the corner of his mouth and he sounds slightly out of breath as he throws open his arms and says: 'Come, my dear foe, let's embrace. I'll crush your bones to powder!'

Make a COMBAT roll at a Difficulty of 15.

Successful COMBAT roll	turn to **310**
Failed COMBAT roll	turn to **253**

291

She climbs up the lifeline like a fat black spider. A claw of a hand reaches up, grey and liver-spotted.

'Help an old lady, then, my dears,' she wheezes.

'Help her be damned!' snarls the mate, brandishing his flensing knife. 'Let me cut her loose. Drowning's a fair fate for such as her.'

Agree to the mate's suggestion	turn to **70**
Pull her up on deck	turn to **89**

292

Someone must have slipped a sleeping powder in your drink, because you wake late with an aching head. Feeling slightly sick, you go straight to your travelling chest. Your worst fears are confirmed – all your cash and possessions are gone.

Make a THIEVERY roll at a Difficulty of 15.

Successful THIEVERY roll	turn to **312**
Failed THIEVERY roll	turn to **329**

293

It will cost you 30 Shards to buy a blessing. Cross off this sum and write Luck in the Blessings box on your Adventure Sheet. The blessing allows you to reroll any one dice result. This needn't necessarily be an ability roll; you could use it to reroll an encounter result that you don't want.

You can have only one Luck blessing at a time, and it will work only once. When you use it, cross it off your Adventure Sheet.

Now turn to **44**.

294

You are transformed into a bird and have no cares other than to soar off with the rest of the flock. After many months, you chance to alight on the deck of a ship and when the other birds fly off you are left behind – human once more. The captain of the vessel listens to your tale with astonishment, but seems to accept it as true. 'I have heard that the natives of the Weeping Jungle believe that all mankind were birds once.' You have not lost your money or possessions, which were transformed with you, but your ship is gone; cross it off your Ship's Manifest. The captain agrees to drop you off in Smogmaw, unless you would rather pay him 30 Shards to take you back to Dweomer.

Disembark at Smogmaw	turn to **44**
Pay 30 Shards to go to Dweomer	turn to **100**

295

The streets of Smogmaw are narrow boardwalks, some of them floating on pontoons out over the sluggish yellow river. The air is hot and sticky like watery treacle. At dusk a sparkling haze crawls out from the jungle, giving this place its name: the Misty Estuary. Roll two dice.

Score 2-4	Press-ganged!	turn to **315**
Score 5-9	A pleasant stroll	turn to **44**
Score 10-12	A mysterious hut	turn to **332**

296

'How can I offer blessings and the like?' laments the priest, a stooped little man with a bald pate and, appropriately enough, a hooked beak of a nose.

'What's the problem?'

'The idol of the god was stolen by unscrupulous people of the Macaw Tribe. Until it is returned, there is no divine power here.'

If you have a **winged idol**, turn to **316**. If not, turn to **44**.

297

The market is held in a warren of booths set up in a roofed arcade at the eastern edge of town. Items with no purchase price are not available locally.

Armour	*To buy*	*To sell*
Leather (Defence +1)	60 Shards	45 Shards
Ring mail (Defence +2)	120 Shards	90 Shards
Chain mail (Defence +3)	240 Shards	180 Shards

Weapons (sword, axe, etc)	*To buy*	*To sell*
No COMBAT bonus	50 Shards	40 Shards
COMBAT bonus +1	250 Shards	200 Shards
COMBAT bonus +2	—	400 Shards

Magical equipment	*To buy*	*To sell*
Amber wand (MAGIC +1)	—	300 Shards

Other items	*To buy*	*To sell*
Compass (SCOUTING +1)	500 Shards	400 Shards
Cross-staff (SCOUTING +2)	900 Shards	700 Shards
Sextant (SCOUTING +3)	1300 Shards	1100 Shards
Lantern	80 Shards	40 Shards
Selenium ore	—	700 Shards

If you have a ship and want to load a cargo of copper ore, you should visit the mines. When you're through here, turn to **99**.

298

'Where to now, skipper?' asks the helmsman as he takes the ship out of Vervayens harbour.

Steer north	turn to **119**
Steer south	turn to **263**
Steer west	turn to **42**
Steer east	turn to **303**

299

A shrieking phantom becomes lodged at the top of the mainmast, where it rants and flickers like a ball of lightning. The mate comes to you with his hair on end and pleads for you to exorcize it before the ship is doomed. Make a SANCTITY roll at a Difficulty of 15.

Successful SANCTITY roll	turn to **280**
Failed SANCTITY roll	turn to **14**

300

Far out at sea with only the stars to guide you, you taste the salty wind and ponder your next course.

Steer west	turn to **370**
Steer east	turn to **153**
Steer north	turn to **208**
Steer south	turn to **468**

301

'Ah!' cries the cook, emerging from the galley to sniff the fresh salt breeze. 'A life on the open waves – what king in his palace could hope for better contentment?'

Recover 1 Stamina point if injured, then roll two dice.

Score 2-3	Pirates	turn to **398**
Score 4-5	Storm	turn to **562**
Score 6-12	An uneventful voyage	turn to **13**

302

Recover 1 Stamina point if injured.

Balmy nights filled with a million stars are followed by days of tranquil beauty. With a good following wind, the ship ploughs on through waves the colour of amethyst. What could disturb your mood of perfect contentment? Roll two dice to find out.

Score 2-4	Pirates	turn to **176**
Score 5-6	Flying fish	turn to **501**
Score 7-9	Nothing	turn to **320**
Score 10-12	A hurricane	turn to **285**

303

The sun's rim dips, the stars rush out – at one stride comes the dark. By the stern lamp you can see the helmsman's face gleaming pale and gaunt. Like all the crew, he senses something uncanny on the air.

'I don't mind admitting it,' mutters the mate, 'fear sips at the blood of my heart as from a frosted cup.'

'Hold steady, mister,' you tell him. 'We must set a stout example for the crew.'

Roll two dice.

Score 2-5	Barnacle men	turn to **80**
Score 6-7	A dreadful doom	turn to **683**
Score 8-9	A skeletal ship	turn to **428**
Score 10-12	The Furies descend	turn to **693**

304

'Ah, this is the life,' declares the bosun as he stretches contentedly in the shade under a palm tree. The exertion in the heat of the afternoon has made you all drowsy. To stay awake you must either have the codeword *Chill* or succeed in a MAGIC roll of Difficulty 12; otherwise you have to take a nap.

| Stay awake | turn to **5** |
| Fall asleep | turn to **582** |

305

Lose the codeword *Cosy*.

They doze off. You shake each man and yell in his ears, but this is an enchanted slumber. You can only wake them if you succeed in a MAGIC roll at a Difficulty of 17.

| Successful MAGIC roll | turn to **45** |
| Failed MAGIC roll | turn to **64** |

306

The pirates pull alongside and cast grappling hooks to seize your vessel. Within moments they are swarming aboard. You offer them your goods, but plead for the freedom of your crew. Make a CHARISMA roll at a Difficulty of 15.

| Successful CHARISMA roll | turn to **416** |
| Failed CHARISMA roll | turn to **435** |

307

You help yourself to the pirates' treasure, which amounts to 150 Shards. Record it on your Adventure Sheet. Their ship's hold contains 1 Cargo Unit of furs, which you can add to your own cargo if your ship has room for it. You can also take the **pirate captain's head** – such a trophy can fetch a good reward in civilized ports.Once you have made the necessary adjustments to your Adventure Sheet, turn to **101**.

308

Unless you have the codeword *Calcium*, lose 1-6 Stamina points (the score of one die) as you vainly struggle for breath in the thin air.

If you survive, you can climb back down to your ship and cut the cable loose before continuing on your way: turn to **228**.

309

'Sail away from dusk and death,' says the glowing image. 'Long before you reach the place of many-headed ones you will encounter a grim stranger. Unarmed you must struggle with him, and three times cast him to the deck; then you can demand your boon.'

The figure vanishes in a spray of wispy green lights. Get the codeword *Certain* and turn to **252**.

310

For the third time in a row, you lift the stranger clear off his feet and smash him hard against the deck. This time he raises his hand in submission.

'Enough. You win,' he says, staggering to his feet. 'You're the strongest there is.'

So saying, he jumps back down to his boat and sails off.

Increase your unwounded Stamina score by 5 points. Also add 1 to COMBAT. Then turn to **125**.

311

You are on the open ocean somewhere north of Braelak, the Sorcerers' Isle.

Steer southwards	turn to **9**
Go west	turn to **129**
Go east	turn to **301**
Head towards the mainland	*Cities of Gold and Glory* **187**

312

It takes a thief to catch a thief. During a thorough search of the ship, you discover a secret compartment behind the cook's bunk where there is a large stash of stolen property.

'My old tobacco pipe!' cries the bosun. He rolls up his sleeves and advances menacingly on the cook. 'You scurvy swab!'

Another sailor is appointed as cook, to general approval. For his many crimes both in and out of the galley, the cook is sent to feed the sharks.

Turn to **154**.

313

You drag yourself up a beach of large pebbles strewn with fronds of seaweed. Lying for a few hours in the weak sunshine goes some way to restoring your strength, and you manage to stagger inland to look for signs of habitation. The landscape is desolate and windswept, but you can see a few sheep grazing on the hillsides.

Turn to **436**.

314

The tavern is just a wooden hut with curtains of woven pandanus leaves serving as partitions. Customers sit or squat on mats on the floor. The place reeks of sharp liquor and pipe smoke.

If you have the codeword *Church*, turn to **331**.

If not, you can get a bed here for 1 Shard a day. Each day you spend resting at the tavern, roll one die.

Score 1	Dysentery; lose 1 Stamina point
Score 2	No gain or loss of Stamina
Score 3-6	A good rest; recover 1 Stamina if injured

When you are ready to leave, turn to **44**.

You lose your way and end up in a quiet spot behind a row of huts, where a half-dozen assailants leap at you. Seconds later you are face down in the rank mud and struggling for your liberty.

To break free and escape you must make a COMBAT roll at a Difficulty of 13.

Successful COMBAT roll	turn to **44**
Failed COMBAT roll	turn to **345**

'This is the very idol of which I spoke!' cries the priest delightedly.

He takes the **winged idol** from you and installs it inside the teepee. Cross it off your list of possessions and get the codeword *Cushat*.

You also have the chance to increase your SCOUTING score by 1 if you can roll higher than your current SCOUTING score on two dice.

After making all necessary adjustments to your Adventure Sheet, turn to **277**.

The hills of Copper Island are honeycombed with mine workings. Beside a tunnel mouth you see a hut where the mine foreman conducts business.

Go to see the foreman	turn to **38**
Enter the mines	turn to **394**
Return to Brazen	turn to **99**

On a small island like this there is not much on sale, but at least the villagers fall over themselves to offer you a bargain.

'Nothing is too good for our saviour!' declares one old lady with grateful tears in her eyes.

Armour	*To buy*	*To sell*
Leather (Defence +1)	free!	40 Shards
Ring mail (Defence +2)	80 Shards	80 Shards
Chain mail (Defence +3)	150 Shards	150 Shards
Splint armour (Defence +4)	–	300 Shards

| **Plate armour (Defence +5)** | – | 700 Shards |
| **Heavy plate (Defence +6)** | – | 1000 Shards |

Weapons (sword, axe, etc)	To buy	To sell
Without COMBAT bonus	free!	40 Shards
COMBAT bonus +1	180 Shards	180 Shards
COMBAT bonus +2	–	280 Shards
COMBAT bonus +3	–	400 Shards

Other items	To buy	To sell
Candle	free!	1 Shard
Rope	free!	30 Shards
Lantern	75 Shards	75 Shards

When you have finished your business here, turn to **20**.

319

The nobles are so impressed by your wit and good manners that they make you a gift of a **courtier's mask**.

'If you should ever visit our land, this will admit you to the highest social circles,' they tell you.

Turn to **78**.

320

You are sailing off the coast of Ankon-Konu just a few leagues north of Smogmaw, the famous trading town that is home to a thousand ne'er-do-wells from all points of the compass.

South to Smogmaw	turn to **266**
North east to Starspike Island	turn to **192**
Due north	turn to **303**
West	turn to **263**
East to the Sea of Hydras	turn to **337**

321

Your ordeal is over. You resolve to leave these bane-drenched waters with all speed.

Go north	turn to **119**

Go south   turn to **302**
Go east   turn to **156**
Go west   turn to **4**

322

You are south of Marlock City – or Old Sokar, to give the port its original name, which still appears on most charts. The helmsman asks for a new bearing.

Steer west   turn to **402**
South   turn to **81**
North   *The War-Torn Kingdom* **222**
East   turn to **66**

323

Obviously a powerful sleep spell permeates this island. You know you can only overcome it by using stronger magic of your own. The song of the mermaids bursts to your lips as a result of sudden inspiration. It has the desired effect – the men rise from the stone couches and follow you like sleepwalkers along the causeway. Turn to **102**.

324

Roll two dice and add your Rank. Add 1 to the total if you have an average crew, 2 if you have a good crew, or 3 if you have an excellent crew.

Score 1-6   The pirates overtake you   turn to **286**
Score 7+   You outrun them   turn to **24**

325

The discovery of a rat's skeleton at the bottom of a used beer barrel provokes discontent among the crew. Matters are worsened by the first mate's jocular remark that the rat will have given the beer some flavour. The men become surly.

At seven bells in the forenoon watch, you come on deck to discover the men on duty have broken a keg of black Barony wine out of ship's stores and are blind drunk. The ship has been drifting untended for hours!

Roll two dice.

Score 2-4   turn to **55**
Score 5-6   turn to **210**
Score 7   turn to **172**
Score 8-9   turn to **246**
Score 10-11   turn to **303**
Score 12   *Lords of the Rising Sun* **309**

326

It is getting harder to breathe; lose 3 Stamina points if you don't have the codeword *Calcium*. If still alive, you see three men of violet hue come dashing at you wielding thin rapiers of unearthly metal. Your stout seamen of Golnir are at your side, leaving you to deal with the leader of these alien skyfarers.

Violet Man, COMBAT 9, Defence 12, Stamina 9

If you turn and flee, they will get a strike at your retreating backs, causing the loss of 1-6 Stamina.

Give up and flee   turn to **308**
Fight on and win   turn to **339**

327

The spectre's face is formed of faint patches of shadow in the green glare. 'From the Nozama to the Grimm, from Hypnos' isle to his black-winged mother's spire – at the heart of this cross you'll find the contentment you seek.'

The light flickers, flares briefly, and goes out. You feel as if you have awakened from a dream. Get the codeword *Covet* and turn to **252**.

328

The serpent is big, but old and slow. The sailors slaughter it easily, one man holding down its head with the end of an oar while the others slice it up with their swords.

The island appears deserted. You return to the ship and give the order to be under way. Turn to **125**.

329

You search high and low, but the stolen items are nowhere to be found. Cross all cash and items off your Adventure Sheet, then turn to **154**.

330

You tell the priestess you no longer want to be an initiate. She utters a long weary sigh and throws her head back in the slumbrous heat. 'Go then.'

'Do I not have to pay compensation? That is customary.'

'Not here in the tropics. Every exertion only makes a pool for flies to paddle in. I cannot be bothered to rise from my divan to open the strongbox. Now, begone.'

Turn to **44**.

331

In one corner you see three of your treacherous former crewmen enjoying a drink. They don't seem to have noticed you. The memory of their mutiny makes your blood seethe.

Attack them	turn to **344**
Speak to them	turn to **35**
Wait and watch	turn to **203**

332

There is a shaman's hut made of sheaves of straw halfway between the shanties at the edge of the town and the wall of dark foliage that marks the start of the jungle. The shaman will trade magical items if you are interested.

Magical equipment	To buy	To sell
Amber wand (MAGIC +1)	500 Shards	350 Shards
Ebony wand (MAGIC +2)	1000 Shards	700 Shards
Cobalt wand (MAGIC +3)	2000 Shards	1500 Shards
Selenium wand (MAGIC +4)	4000 Shards	3000 Shards
Celestium wand (MAGIC +5)	–	4500 Shards

Other items	To buy	To sell
Faery mead	–	400 Shards
Silver horseshoe	–	200 Shards
Hydra's tooth	1250 Shards	750 Shards
Four-leaf clover	–	100 Shards
Witch's hand	300 Shards	150 Shards

Scroll of Ebron	–	350 Shards
Sea-green lens	–	100 Shards
Spectral veil	500 Shards	200 Shards
Selenium ore	–	600 Shards

Where there is no purchase price, the item is not in stock. When you have concluded your business with the shaman, turn to **44**.

333

If you have the title Unspeakable Cultist, turn to **346**. If not, turn to **18**.

334

The Motherlode Inn offers a pallet and one square meal for 2 Shards a day. Each day you spend here you can recover 1 Stamina point if injured. When you are ready to leave, turn to **99**.

335

You put your feet up at the house provided for you by the grateful islanders. You can rest here as long as you want, so if injured you can now restore your Stamina to its normal unwounded score. You can also leave money and possessions here to save carrying them around. Record in the box anything you are leaving. Each time you return, roll two dice.

ITEMS KEPT AT HOUSE

Score 2-9   Everything just as you left it
Score 10-12   A fire destroyed your possessions
When you are finished here, choose where to go now.

Visit the market	turn to **318**
Consult the wise woman	turn to **390**
Upgrade your crew	turn to **349**
Put to sea	turn to **298**

336

A gilded pleasure barge sails by, bearing noblemen from Aku to Metriciens. They pull alongside to converse with you for a short while before proceeding on their way.

Make a CHARISMA roll at a Difficulty of 13.

Successful CHARISMA roll	turn to **319**
Failed CHARISMA roll	turn to **78**

337

'The Sea of Hydras,' the navigator says, pointing to the east.

'Why is it so called?' asks the cabin boy in a tone of wonder.

The navigator gives a derisive snort of laughter. 'Need you ask?' Roll two dice.

Score 2-6	A ship from distant lands	turn to **538**
Score 7-9	An uneventful day's sailing	turn to **3**
Score 10-12	An emergency arises	turn to **556**

338

You put ashore to take on fresh water. The crewmen are happy to cavort along the wide golden beach and explore the orchid scented jungle – until the ship's priest comes staggering back with his throat slashed, gurgles 'Iambic pentameter' and dies at your feet.

'Pentameter – that's a sort of ship, like a quinquireme,' says the first mate. 'Iambic, though? Out of a port called Iambus? Where's that?'

The rest of the shore party are spooked. They want to leave.

Set sail at once	turn to **41**
Explore the island	turn to **8**

339

Gasping for breath, your men make a hasty search of the cabin, finding three **swords (COMBAT +1)** and a **fretwork key**.

One of the two men is reeling by now. 'I can't stand it much longer, skipper…' he says.

Explore further along the passage	turn to **29**
Return to your ship	turn to **308**

340

A search is organized and the stowaway is soon found. He is a little dwarf with narrow black eyes who ducks between your legs, runs up on deck and dives into the sea. As you watch him swim away with surprisingly powerful strokes, the first mate brings bad news: 'He broke a hole in the hull. We're sinking!'

You have no choice but to abandon ship. Cross off your ship and crew; you will never see them again. Clinging to an empty barrel, you are swept away by the current and eventually washed up on an island.

Turn to **313**.

341

Lose the codeword *Coracle*.

You put into a bay on a small uncharted island. Going ashore to replenish your supplies, you come across a huge serpent with skin like tree-bark lying in the shade of the trees. It watches you with cold intensity.

'Shall we kill it, skipper?' asks the master of arms.

Have the men attack it	turn to **328**
Kill it yourself	turn to **211**
Leave without disturbing it	turn to **125**

342

You climb back up the sinkhole and hurry away from the Gorgons' lair. What now?

Put to sea in one of the fishing boats	turn to **411**
Cross to the other side of the island	turn to **449**
Pray to your god for deliverance	turn to **467**

343

A clap of her hands brings two more slave boys scurrying over with a card table. A second divan is placed for you to recline. Goblets of chilled fruit juice are set beside you.

If you have a **deck of marked cards** you have the option to use them in the game. Otherwise you will have to play with the priestess's deck.

Use **deck of marked cards** turn to **15**
Agree to play with her deck turn to **34**

344

You plant yourself beside the mat where they're sitting. 'Get up, you dogs, so I can whip you off to hell.'

They get unsteadily to their feet, all the worse for drink. 'Aye, aye, skipper,' says your former mate, Mister Fryer. 'And we'll be happy to take you with us.'

If you have the codeword *Aid* turn to **112**.

Otherwise turn to **73**.

345

You are coshed and dragged aboard a Sokaran merchant ship, the *Tidy Sum*. By the time you come round the ship has already put to sea. You also discover that the press-gang took all your cash (cross it off your Adventure Sheet), though at least they left your possessions.

If you had a ship at Smogmaw, turn to **17**. If not, turn to **36**.

346

The other cultists nod as you enter. 'May His name never be spoken,' they intone in ritual greeting.

'Whose name? Shush!' you reply in the words of the time-honoured catechism.

It is almost time for supper. If you have a **pirate captain's head** or a **witch's hand** to add to the simmering stew, the other cultists present you with a prize medallion worth 200 Shards.

After having your loathsome meal, you slip furtively back to town. Turn to **44**.

347

The only temple in Brazen is consecrated to Molhern. It is a low stone building, artfully fashioned to reflect the style of ancient menhirs.

The priest cannot induct you into the inner mysteries of Molhern's worship. 'I am not senior enough for that, but I can grant blessings.'

If you have the title Illuminate of Molhern, turn to **517**. If not, turn to **498**.

348

To keep the crew busy you set them to making a thorough inspection of the ship. It is soon discovered that someone has been breaking into the food supplies. You have a stowaway on board.

If you have the codeword *Baluster*, turn to **49**. If not, turn to **120**.

349

Half the young men of Vervayens are eager to ship with you, so you have no trouble getting a good stock of volunteers. If your crew quality is poor, upgrade it to average. You cannot get better crew than this on such a small island.

'What now, skipper?' asks your new cabin boy.

Visit the market	turn to **318**
Consult the wise woman	turn to **390**
Go to your house	turn to **335**
Put to sea	turn to **298**

350

The stowaway is a runaway slave who has spent his whole life at sea. He has no money, but in return for letting him stay aboard till you reach port he helps teach your crew what he knows of seafaring. Increase your crew quality by one step (i.e. from poor to average, average to good, or good to excellent). Now turn to **78**.

351 ☐☐☐

You are limited to three new lives from the grove on the Island of Rebirth. If at least one of the three boxes above is blank, put a tick in it and then turn to **69**. When the three boxes are all ticked, you cannot return to life again here.

352

Looking south, you can see the shoreline of Ankon-Konu as a faint mauve line beneath a sky of cobalt blue.

Go south	*The Lone and Level Sands* **100**
Go north	turn to **370**
Go east	turn to **117**
Go west	turn to **40**

353

You tie yourself to the wheel and stand steadfast as the sweet singing of the mermaids wafts across the water. It sounds so lovely, so ethereally unattainable, that you have a wild impulse to hurl yourself into the sea and drift down to meet with the maidens on the sea bed. You even find yourself untying the knots, and you have to punch your fingers against the wheel to make them sore and numb so that you cannot get free.

The ordeal is indescribable. It is like hearing the dying song of your true love, like climbing to the verge of paradise only to slip away at the last instant, like the last day of childhood's innocence…

It ends at last. The crewmen come back on deck with ashen faces. The bosun tells you that you are weeping – you hadn't noticed. He unties the knots and you stagger below, for a while inconsolable. Get the codeword *Cerumen* and turn to **300**.

354

The approaching vessel announces her hostile intent by hoisting the baleful red pennant of the Reavers. Her oars give her a good burst of speed over short distances, and she is soon bearing down on you.

Make a run for it	turn to **324**
Parley	turn to **306**
Fight it out	turn to **286**

355

The sky is the colour of thunder. From behind the clouds comes the muttering of a great storm. The sailors chatter in fear. 'It is the voice of Elnir,' says the cook. 'And he ain't inviting us to dance no blessed jig!'

If you have a blessing of Safety from Storms, you can ignore the storm; cross off the blessing and turn to **648**.

Otherwise the storm hits with titanic fury, tossing huge waves across the deck. Roll one die if your ship is a barque, two dice if it is a brigantine, or three dice if a galleon. Add 1 to the roll if you have an excellent crew; subtract 1 if you have a poor crew.

Score 0-4	Your ship sinks	turn to **486**
Score 5-6	The mast splits	turn to **718**
Score 7-19	You weather the storm	turn to **262**

356

The strange women come closer and one of them touches your face with her long dry fingers. Immediately her crowing laughter turns to a strangled cry of alarm: 'Warm living flesh! Our power did not work, my sister–!'

You take advantage of her surprise to deal her a vicious blow that lays her senseless. Now you have only one of them to fight.

Gorgon, COMBAT 4, Defence 5, Stamina 8

If you win, turn to **393**.

357

Originally there were three gods, those who created the world. These are hardly mentioned in the legends. They are dim, shadowy figures of a primordial age. Even their names bespeak dream-like obscurity: Harkun, He Who Is Like Harkun, and The Third God.

These three having died, their place was taken by powerful demiurges, each with his or her own delineated jurisdiction. Thus there is Tyrnai, overseer of war; Elnir, lord of the sky; irascible Maka, who brings disease and famine if not appeased with sacrifices; Lacuna, lady of the hunt; Nagil, king of the dead; wise Molhern, deity of craftsmen; Sig, who guides the soft footsteps of thieves; the Three Fortunes, goddesses of destiny; and the twin gods Alvir and Valmir, who rule the land under the waves.

Those, at least, are the gods of the northern continent; other countries have their own beliefs. Only a simpleton clings to the concept of one absolute truth.

Turn to **368**.

358

On the far side of a cavern you find three copper doors. To open them you will need a **verdigris key**.

Open a door	turn to **395**
Turn back	turn to **633**

359

'How about that money I put into your business venture?' you ask him.

'Oh yes,' he says, 'that.'

Roll two dice, and add 1 to the dice roll if you are an initiate of the Three Fortunes.

Score 2-4   Loss of 20%
Score 5-6   Loss of 10%
Score 7-8   Profit of 10%
Score 9-11   Profit of 20%
Score 12-13 Profit of 25%

Now turn to **652** and withdraw the sum noted in the box there after adjusting it according to the result rolled.

360

By the time the ship has reversed course, the poor surgeon is no longer in sight. 'He's been swept away to the sea gods' hall,' says the bosun in a voice of great lament.

'What will we do without a surgeon?' says the second mate. 'Now I'll have to wait till we get to Dweomer to get my hair cut.'

Your confidence in your sailing skills has been badly shaken. Lose 1 from your SCOUTING score and turn to **22**.

361

The ship lurches with the impact. Timbers groan and crack. Pirates pour over the rail with a lusty yell, eager on seasoning your decks with blood.

Roll three dice if you are a Warrior, or two dice if you belong to any other profession. Add your Rank to this roll. Then, if your crew is poor quality, subtract 2 from the total. If the crew is good, add 2. If the crew is excellent, add 3.

Score 0-4	Calamity; you are killed	turn to **123**
Score 5-9	Crushing defeat; lose 2-12 Stamina	turn to **435**
Score 10-13	Forced to give in; lose 1-6 Stamina	turn to **416**
Score 14-17	The pirates withdraw	turn to **311**
Score 18+	Outright victory	turn to **379**

362

The moon is a dim patch behind the clouds, as if seen through smoked

glass. Sentries patrol the fortress walls. You will need to make a
THIEVERY roll at a Difficulty of 13 to sneak into the pirate base
undetected.

Successful THIEVERY roll   turn to **690**

Failed THIEVERY roll   turn to **114**

363

The Reavers notice the medallion that hangs from your neck. One of
them steps forward. His bow to the King is clumsy because his stance
is skewed by an old back injury, but he speaks with great eloquence:
'Once a great service was done me by this seafarer. When sore-pressed
by Sokaran warships, the god Sig saw fit to send me a saviour. That
saviour, O King, was the one who stands before you now – one to
whom I pledged to give aid whenever it was needed.'

The King would probably rather torture you to death, but Verin
Crookback is highly respected among the Reavers. You are granted
your freedom. Turn to **656**.

364

You slam open the door and go marching straight up to Lauria's table.
Ignoring her companion, you launch straight into a rant which
eloquently expresses your feelings towards her. You don't trouble with
niceties; your oaths and curses are such that even the shameless Lauria
starts to blush.

Her elderly companion removes his monocle and peers at you in
amazement.

'Look, this just won't do,' he says.

You turn to give him a piece of your mind too, but you find yourself
staring at a treetrunk covered in blue moss –

You look all around. What happened to the tavern? All of a sudden
you're in the middle of a dense forest! Turn to **697**.

365

The matter is judged a draw. Neither you nor Talanexor are satisfied,
but you must abide by the local duelling code. You stomp off without
speaking a word to each other.

Turn to **571**.

366

Rocks rain down like cannon shells, but you are safely clear of the island and they only throw up plumes of spray far astern. You hold off the shore until the eruption is spent. After a night turned to hellish twilight by the flaming torrents of lava, the volcano lapses back into peaceful slumber.

'Jiarosh is content,' says the shaman. 'We can return and rebuild our homes.'

Filled with gratitude for your help, the shaman rewards you with a blessing of Safety from Storms if you don't have one already. Note this on your Adventure Sheet and then turn to **479**.

367

He is happy to have a companion on his quest. You tell your men to take the ship to Yellowport, where you will join them later. Then you climb up behind him and fly off.

The sea whips past far below, then you are over the coast and speeding north. Glimpsed through wispy cloud, the farms and villages look like toys.

The horse rears – you don't know why. Realizing he is losing control of his mount, the hero urges it closer to the ground.

You can see the treetops when suddenly you slip from the saddle and fall. You crash through branches; leaves whip across your face. Then you hit the ground.

Lose 2-12 Stamina points (the roll of two dice). If still alive, you look up but there is no sign of the horse or its rider. Note on your Ship's Manifest that the ship is at Yellowport and then turn to **596** in *The War-Torn Kingdom*.

368

The college library contains thousands of dusty tomes. Few of them have been properly catalogued.

'There's something written about just about anything you could mention,' says the librarian, sweeping his hand along the stacks.

You peer towards the end of the room – except that it hasn't got one. 'Er… the stacks look as if they go on for ever,' you say.

The librarian nods. 'They do. It's a simple infinity spell.'

Pay your library fees of 50 Shards and then make a MAGIC roll at a Difficulty of 15 to see if you can find the book that you're after.

    Successful MAGIC roll   turn to **386**

    Failed MAGIC roll or unable to pay fees   turn to **607**

369

The forest is inhabited by a malevolent unseen spirit that is slowly leeching your life-energy. Lose 1 point from all your abilities (CHARISMA, COMBAT, MAGIC, etc). No ability can go lower than 1. In addition, you lose 1-6 Stamina points (the roll of one die).

You realize you must muster a burst of effort to break out of the wood before you are lost for ever. Make a SCOUTING roll at a Difficulty of 17.

    Successful SCOUTING roll   turn to **705**

    Failed SCOUTING roll   turn to **388**

370

The ship drifts along in a gentle wind. The slow creak of the ship's timbers and the fluttering of the sails makes a sound that lulls you off to sleep at night. Recover 1 Stamina point if injured, then roll two dice.

Score 2-5	Nightmares become real	turn to **204**
Score 6-8	An uneventful journey	turn to **22**
Score 9-12	Man overboard!	turn to **478**

371

Cross off the **selenium ore**. In its place you now have a **selenium wand (MAGIC +4)**. Turn to **262**.

372

The villagers are furiously angry at you for taking advantage of their goodwill. You are pelted first with rotten fruit, then with cobblestones prised up from the streets. Lose 1-6 Stamina points (the score of one die). If you survive that, you rejoin your ship. The plank is hauled up and you hastily cast off. Lose the title Saviour of Vervayens Isle and turn to **298**.

373

The pirates pull alongside and cast grappling hooks to seize your vessel. Within moments they are swarming aboard. You offer them your goods, but plead for the freedom of your crew. Make a CHARISMA roll at a Difficulty of 15.

Successful CHARISMA roll	turn to **431**
Failed CHARISMA roll	turn to **435**

374

You forgot you were standing at the end of the headland. You take a step back, lose your footing, and fall to your death on the sharp rocks below. Turn to **123**.

375

The Mannekyn People are a race of small winged folk. Their home is in the high caves of Sky Mountain, but some have taken up residence among humankind. One such is the famous Tekshin, whose tavern is a favourite halt for travellers on the road from Wheatfields to Haggart's Corner. Turn to **368**.

376

There is nothing of interest on the trau's body but a **pickaxe (COMBAT +2)**. Turn to **358**.

377

There is a sparkle of green light in the gloom. Bending down, you find a **sea-green lens**. Who could have dropped that? One of the miners? You drop the **sea-green lens** into your pocket; note it on your list of possessions and then turn to **396**.

378

The crewmen are too drunk to take any notice of your orders.

`Shtop bleatin' an' have yourself a li'l drink!' declares the cabin boy boldly, brandishing a bottle of wine in your face.

You give him a sound buffet for his impertinence and then try to think what to do. You can't sail the ship single-handed. But what if the Reavers turn up while your crew are in this hopeless state?

Wait till they sober up	turn to **397**
Leave and travel on foot	turn to **417**

379

The pirates' treasure comprises 900 Shards, which you can record on your Adventure Sheet. Their ship's hold contains 1 Cargo Unit of textiles, which you can add to your own cargo if you have room for it. Your mate suggests taking the **pirate captain's head** in case it carries a bounty.

You also get a chance to increase in Rank after your stirring leadership in battle. Roll two dice, and if the result is greater than your current Rank then you gain a Rank. You also gain 1-6 Stamina points permanently: increase your normal (unwounded) Stamina score by the roll of one die. Remember that going up in Rank increases your Defence.

Once you have made the necessary adjustments to your Adventure Sheet, turn to **311**.

380

You stow away in the hold of one of the pirate ships and wait for her to put to sea. Attempt a THIEVERY roll at Difficulty 16 to see if you can avoid being discovered.

Successful THIEVERY roll	turn to **419**
Failed THIEVERY roll	turn to **114**

381

A ship comes alongside showing the banner of the High King: a golden starburst on a field of azure blue.

`Long live the King!' cries your helmsman, a gruff old Harkunan who at heart is a wild romantic.

If you have the codeword *Diamond*, turn to **676**. If not, turn to **490**.

382

'Ah,' says Lauria as you approach her table. 'I don't think I had the chance to introduce my father the last time you were here...'

You bow to him. 'Sir.'

'Father is the Warden of All Hellions College,' says Lauria.

You'll get further playing it cool this time. 'Are you aware,' you ask Lauria, 'that because of you I was whipped half to death? Look, I still bear the scars.'

'Please,' says her father, 'I do not care to have you expose yourself to me over dinner. And in any case, those can hardly be called scars.'

He traces his finger over your injuries, which heal completely. Add 1 to your CHARISMA.

'There,' sighs Lauria. 'Now perhaps you'll stop being such a pest.' But she says it with a smile.

Lose the codeword *Anger* and turn to **571**.

383

Talanexor concedes defeat rather than suffer the full effect of your conjurations. A tribunal finds him guilty of besmirching your good name and orders him to pay you 500 Shards by way of compensation. As he counts out the money he gives you a glowering look and says under his breath: 'You'll lie in your grave before you can spend the last of these coins. See if you can deflect that curse!'

He turns and strides away. Get the codeword *Cheese* and turn to **571**.

384

The terrified islanders swarm about your ship. Women and children are put in the hold, and any cargo you had is jettisoned (cross it off the Ship's Manifest). Others must cling to the rigging or perch on the rail. The extra load makes the ship float alarmingly low in the water.

As you put out from the shore, the volcano is already starting to spit out long fiery torrents of lava. But the danger isn't over yet.

Roll one die. Subtract 1 if your ship is a barque; add 1 if it is a galleon.

Score 0-2	The ship capsizes	turn to **486**
Score 3-7	Luck is with you	turn to **366**

You manage to convince the hero that it would be unwise to face the gods. 'Men have been stricken with madness for such prideful folly,' you remind him.

He agrees at last. 'In that case I must return to the enchantress who lent me this marvellous steed, back in Atticala. Do you wish to join me?'

'What of my ship?'

'You go ahead and enjoy yourself, skipper,' says the first mate. 'We'll meet up with you in Port Skios.'

Go with the horseman — *Legions of the Labyrinth* **66**

Decline his offer — turn to **135**

386

What are you interested in finding out about?

The Bluewood	turn to **573**
The key of stars	turn to **591**
Estragon	turn to **609**
The Feathered Lands	turn to **627**
Akatsurai	turn to **645**
The gods	turn to **357**
Ghosts	turn to **247**
Trau	turn to **663**
Mannekyn People	turn to **375**
The Uttakin	turn to **681**
Old Harkuna	turn to **698**
The Innis Shoals	turn to **2**
The city of Dangor	turn to **650**
The Shadar	turn to **668**
The Forest of Larun	turn to **542**
Mermaids	turn to **63**

387

You climb back down the cliff to the beach. If you have a ship docked at the southern bay on Sorcerers' Isle, turn to **122**. If not, you have no option but to climb back up and try to make your way through the Bluewood to Dweomer – turn to **407**.

388

You look back. The path you came along is not there any more. You are lost in the Bluewood.

To find your way out again you will need to make a SCOUTING roll at a Difficulty of 15.

Successful SCOUTING roll	turn to **705**
Failed SCOUTING roll	turn to **369**

389

It is possible to forge a powerful wand with this substance, but if the alloy is not prepared using exactly the right mixture then the ore could decay explosively. To make the attempt you require a MAGIC roll at

Difficulty 16 – though you may prefer to leave well enough alone.

Successful MAGIC roll	turn to **371**
Failed MAGIC roll	turn to **708**
Don't attempt it	turn to **262**

390

The wise woman lives a reclusive existence. Her home is a cave in the cliffs high above the village. The islanders turn to her for medicine, soothsaying and the favour of the gods.

She greets you with a sticky yellow smile and waits for you to fill her hand with silver. For 5 Shards she will give you a blessing of Safety from Storms. Note this in the Blessings box on your Adventure Sheet if you decide to buy it. You can have only one Safety from Storms blessing at a time, and it will work only once.

When you have finished your business here, turn to **335**.

391

Sailors believe that at times like this it is possible to whistle up a wind. Make a MAGIC roll at a Difficulty of 14 (Difficulty 12 if you are an initiate of Alvir and Valmir) to see if you have the knack.

Successful MAGIC roll	turn to **155**
Failed MAGIC roll	turn to **624**

392

The pirates smash their craft against yours and come scuttling across the boarding ladders like big black spiders.

Roll three dice if you are a Warrior, or two dice if you belong to any other profession. Add your Rank to this roll.

Then, if your crew is poor quality, subtract 2 from the total. If the crew is good quality, add 2. If the crew is excellent quality, add 3.

Score 0-4	Calamity; you are killed	turn to **123**
Score 5-9	Crushing defeat; lose 2-12 Stamina	turn to **435**
Score 10-13	Forced to give in; lose 1-6 Stamina	turn to **416**
Score 14-17	The pirates withdraw	turn to **648**
Score 18+	Outright victory	turn to **412**

393

With the Gorgons dead, the curse is lifted and the villagers come back to life. When they realize you have rescued them, they swear to honour you for ever.

You are feasted for days on end and can recover any lost Stamina points. Then the villagers come to you and say they have another gift – a ship, crewed by the young men of the island. They are eager to sail with you and seek adventure.

Note on your Ship's Manifest that you have a brigantine (cargo capacity: 2 Cargo Units) with an average quality crew. Also note the title Saviour of Vervayens Isle on your Adventure Sheet. Turn to **298**.

394

A tunnel winds down steeply from the mine entrance and then forks in two. Rough steps have been hacked into the floor. The rock is so hard that there is almost no need for timbers to shore up the roof.

Go to the surface	turn to **25**
Take the left-hand tunnel	turn to **414**
Take the right-hand tunnel	turn to **434**

395

If you are using a **candle** to light your way, cross it off as it cannot be used again. Now choose which door you will open. Each is a magical portal leading to a distant place. Note that if you do not have *The War-Torn Kingdom* or *The Plains of Howling Darkness*, which are other books in this series, you had better open the right-hand door.

The left-hand door	*The War-Torn Kingdom* **670**
The middle door	*The Plains of Howling Darkness* **85**
The right-hand door	turn to **415**

396

You can take a **pickaxe** and a lump of **copper ore**. There is nothing else to interest you here, so when you are ready to leave turn to **394**.

397

Sure enough, just a few hours later, the door of the tavern flies open and a pack of cutthroats come storming in. Most of your crewmen are in no fit state to fight, but you manage to rally a few of them. Roll two dice (three if you're a Warrior) and add your Rank. Add 2 to the total if your crew is excellent quality.

Score 3-7	You are killed	turn to **123**
Score 8-12	You are captured	turn to **454**
Score 13+	You win	turn to **455**

398

You are close-hauled and making slow progress against a contrary wind when another vessel appears off the port bow. She is bearing hard in, and the crew gasp in dismay as they sight the fluttering red pennants of the Reavers.

Make a run for it	turn to **418**
Parley	turn to **456**
Fight it out	turn to **474**

399

The narrow Straits of Alvir permit safe passage between the Sea of Stilts and the Violet Ocean, assuming you are a skilled enough mariner to steer your vessel through.

Attempt a SCOUTING roll at Difficulty 14.

If you succeed, turn to paragraph **220** in *The Isle of a Thousand Spires*. Otherwise, you are forced back – turn to **40**

400

The Reaver King regards you with a baleful half-smile. 'How proudly you stand there before me. Are you not aware that I hold your fate in my hands?'

He steps forward as though to embrace you, then suddenly brings his fist up in a vicious punch to the gut. You double up, gasping for breath. Lose 1 Stamina point. If still alive, you hear him say: 'The only question is whether to kill you at once or have a little fun first.'

If you have a **silver medallion**, turn to **363**. If not, turn to **638**.

401

Lauria goes through a doorway. A few moments later an upstairs light comes on and you see her outlined against the window pane. You glance around to find out the name of this street, but you can hardly see ten paces because of the dense fog.

The light goes out. You wait outside until Lauria must be asleep, then you let yourself into the house and tiptoe upstairs. Make a THIEVERY roll at Difficulty 13.

Successful THIEVERY roll	turn to **421**
Failed THIEVERY roll	turn to **514**

402

'I don't like it, skipper,' says the pilot, gazing at the charts. 'We're steering betwixt Death and the wine-dark sea.'

Arrant superstition. You will have none of it. Roll two dice.

Score 2-4	Pirates	turn to **511**
Score 5	Storm	turn to **580**
Score 6-8	An uneventful voyage	turn to **32**
Score 9-12	A ghost ship	turn to **530**

403

The ship plunges on as though hauled by sea demons. Indeed, some of your crew even claim to have caught glimpses of such creatures, which they say resemble giant horses with manes of green froth plunging neck-deep through the sea.

Roll two dice. Subtract 1 from the result if your ship is a barque; add 1 if she is a galleon.

Score 1-6	Abandon ship!	turn to **486**
Score 7-13	The tempest passes	turn to **468**

404

You raise your arms to the volcano and plead with the god Jiarosh to stay his wrath. Make a SANCTITY roll at a Difficulty of 14.

Successful SANCTITY roll	turn to **425**
Failed SANCTITY roll	turn to **444**

405

Targdaz's horse flies you back to your castle in a matter of hours.

'I didn't want to waste the spell,' he says as it flies off. 'Each time I summon that steed it costs a year of my life.'

You are more concerned about your ship and crew. Make a
CHARISMA roll at a Difficulty of 13. Success means that the crew
followed your orders and you can note that the ship is now docked at
the port of your choice. Failure means they sailed off and you must
cross the vessel's details off your Ship's Manifest.

Now turn to **20** in *The Court of Hidden Faces*.

406

If you possess a **ship's deeds**, turn to **710**. Otherwise read on.

There is one ship for sale. She is a barque with a carrying capacity of
1 Cargo Unit; she will cost you 320 Shards.

'What about the crew?' you ask the man who is selling her.

'Men from Marmorek,' he says. 'Landlubbers every one of them,
but they're willing to learn.'

If you decide to buy the ship, remember to cross off the money and
record the details on the Ship's Manifest. The Crew Quality is poor.
Remember to change the entry in the Docked column each time you
arrive at a new port; it is currently docked at Dweomer, of course.

Now turn to **100**.

407

You are at the top of high cliffs swathed in mist. Nearby stands a gloomy
tower. Looking north, you are faced by the impenetrable mass of the

Bluewood, that trackless forest from whose bourne few travellers return except as mindless shrieking zombies with a ravening thirst for human blood…

No, no; that's just an old wives' tale. Or so you tell yourself.

Venture into the Bluewood	turn to **697**
Go to the tower	turn to **426**
Descend the cliffs	turn to **387**

408

If you have a **witch's hand**, turn to **555**. Otherwise, turn to **388**.

409

A chunk of **selenium ore** is discovered embedded in a coral reef. It is still hot from its fall, causing the sea to hiss each time a wave laps over it.

'Heaven must be hotter than hell,' is the bosun's eminently scientific conjecture based on the evidence.

Note the **selenium ore** on your Adventure Sheet. If you are an initiate of Molhern, turn to **389**. Otherwise turn to **262**.

410

The captain rewards you with the contents of his hold: 2 Cargo Units of metals. Note these on your Ship's Manifest, assuming you have the space to load them aboard. (You can jettison your current cargo to make room, if you wish.)

'What will you do now?' you ask the captain.

He gives a quick bray of exhausted laughter. 'Get my ship into port, sell her, and use the money to buy a tavern. I'll never put to sea again, that's for sure.'

Turn to **137**.

411

The boats are badly weathered, having been left untended for a long time. You choose the most seaworthy and wait until the tide is in to float her out of the harbour, preferring to cast yourself on the mercy of the sea than risk a night on this eerie island. Roll one die.

Score 1-2	Wrecked on a beach	turn to **505**

| Score 3-4 | Picked up by pirates | turn to **472** |
| Score 5-6 | Reach the mainland | turn to **430** |

412

The pirates' treasure amounts to 1200 Shards and their ship's hold contains 1 Cargo Unit of spices, which you can add to your own cargo if you have room for it. Your mate also thinks you should take the **pirate captain's head** as a trophy.

You also get a chance to increase in Rank. Roll two dice, and if the result is greater than your current Rank then you gain a Rank. You also gain 1-6 Stamina points permanently: increase your normal (unwounded) Stamina score by the roll of one die. Remember that going up in Rank will increase your Defence by 1.

Once you have made the necessary adjustments to your Adventure Sheet, turn to **648**.

413

If you have a **treasure map**, turn to **132**. If not, turn to **150**.

414

No daylight penetrates this far below ground. In order to proceed you must have a **candle, lantern** or other source of light. Otherwise you have no choice but to turn back.

| Proceed along the tunnel | turn to **452** |
| Turn back | turn to **317** |

415

You emerge from a doorway set in the side of a tree. You now seem to be standing in a forest. The foliage overhead is so thick that you can hardly tell if it is day or night.

Turn to **697**.

416

The pirates take your cargo, all your possessions and your cash. They also seize your ship for themselves – cross all these off your Ship's Manifest and Adventure Sheet.

They are convinced it is worth leaving you alive, at least.

'Yes, that way we can prey on you again in future,' says their leader with a feral grin. 'Every good fisherman knows to throw some of his catch back!'

You are put off in Dweomer. As the pirates sail off, you vow revenge. Turn to **100**.

417

Get the codeword *Colour* and then turn to **436**.

418

Roll two dice and add your Rank. Add 1 to the total if you have an average crew, 2 if you have a good crew, or 3 if you have an excellent crew.

Score 1-6	The pirates overtake you	turn to **474**
Score 7+	You outrun them	turn to **13**

419

After several weeks at sea, the ship puts in at Smogmaw. You wait until the pirates are carousing in town before slipping away, taking with you 50 Shards from their coffers for good measure!

Lose the codeword *Colour* if you have it and turn to **44**.

420

Amcha sleeps in a chamber at the rear of his throne room. He has no personal guards – that would suggest weakness, and he is a proud man. But there are regular patrols of sentries around the citadel.

Make a THIEVERY roll at a Difficulty of 14 to sneak in and do the deed without being apprehended.

Successful THIEVERY roll	turn to **585**
Failed THIEVERY roll	turn to **493**

421

You could never normally sneak in on a master thief like Lauria, but after a heavy meal of venison and roast parsnips washed down with cider she is sleeping as soundly as a gorged vampire at noonday.

Rob her	turn to **440**
Kidnap her	turn to **459**

422

Black clouds boil up suddenly across a clear sky. Within minutes the ship is bucking wildly in an icy gale as sheets of lightning crackle overhead. 'No natural storm could come up so quick,' says the bosun. 'This is sorcery.'

Assuming he's right, you can try to cancel the storm by making a MAGIC roll at a Difficulty of 14.

Successful MAGIC roll	turn to **226**
Failed MAGIC roll	turn to **403**

423

With a heart full of sadness, you watch your ship drop out of sight beyond the horizon. Cross her details off your Ship's Manifest.

Rowing on with dogged perseverance, you wait for the Three Fortunes to deal you another hand. Roll one die.

Score 1-2	Wrecked on a beach	turn to **505**
Score 3-4	Picked up by pirates	turn to **472**
Score 5-6	Reach the mainland	turn to **430**

424

The rider is an adventurer from Atticala, the land that lies across the Sea of Stilts.

'I am flying to the top of Sky Mountain,' he declares, 'where I expect to confront the gods themselves!'

Ask to go with him	turn to **367**
Advise him not to go	turn to **385**
Bid him farewell	turn to **135**

425

Jiarosh hears and heeds your prayers. The groundshocks die down. The smoke blows away on the wind. All is quiet.

The villagers are jubilant. 'You are a mighty shaman,' they say. 'Honour us by staying here as our guest.'

Stay on the island	turn to **706**
Set to sea	turn to **479**

426

You peer into the translucent walls of the tower, but it is like looking into a deep green pond. You can make out nothing of what lies within.

Entering, you find a winding staircase which you climb to a landing. All the way you are beset by tiny stinging creatures; lose 1-6 Stamina points (the score of one die).

Leave the tower	turn to **407**
Press on up the staircase	turn to **680**

427

The men raise three cheers as you get hold of the surgeon under one arm and swim back to the ship. When he has somewhat recovered, the surgeon administers himself a measure of brandy 'for medicinal purposes'.

You are the hero of the hour. Roll two dice, and if the total is higher than your CHARISMA score you can increase it by 1.

After making any necessary adjustments to your Adventure Sheet, turn to **22**.

428

The first mate rushes into your cabin one day towards dusk. Deep in calculation over your charts, you barely glance up when he blurts out: 'Captain, an ancient hulk has drifted alongside.'

'She's adrift, you say? A derelict?'

'No derelict,' he replies in an agitated voice, 'She has a skeleton crew!'

'Hmm.' You sit back, folding your arms behind your head. 'Perhaps her skipper wants to flesh out his crew with some of our men...'

'I think you're right!' cries the mate, staring past you with wild eyes.

Something is tapping on the window pane — something that has terrified the mate. You turn to see what it is. A host of ivory faces are leering in through the casement-window. It is a skeleton crew indeed! Crashing through the glass, the bony sailors leap among you chittering in ghastly glee.

Fight them	turn to **539**
Drive them off with prayer	turn to **575**
Cast yourself at their mercy	turn to **447**

429

The wind dies away, leaving the sails sagging. At first the crew jokes about getting a break from duties, but days turn to weeks and the wind does not pick up. All around the sea lies as flat as a mirror. The mood of the crew is grim; many wonder if they will die here, out of sight of land.

You take a drink of water from the barrel on deck. It is the last cupful. Without a wind you are surely doomed. You and your officers could strike out for the mainland in the cutter, but that would mean abandoning the rest of the men.

Whistle a tune	turn to **391**
Abandon ship in the cutter	turn to **520**
Stay with your crewmen	turn to **590**

430

By the time you arrive at a port you are ankle-deep in water and exhausted from your ordeal. You stumble out of the boat, which goes listing off with the current, and wearily make your way towards the town. Turn to **44**.

431

The pirates take your cargo, your personal belongings and any cash you have on board. To your surprise, they agree to leave you with your ship.

'In truth, it's not worth the effort of hauling back home,' remarks the pirate captain acerbically as he goes back aboard his own vessel.

You watch them sail away. Amend your Adventure Sheet and Ship's Manifest, then turn to **648**.

432

The Gorgons go to their beds only once the moon has set. You peer down at them in the faint lamplight. While they doze, their ophidian tresses sway drowsily on the pillows. Make a SCOUTING roll at a Difficulty of 10.

Successful SCOUTING roll	turn to **451**
Failed SCOUTING roll	turn to **469**

433

Instead of the idyllic garden you found on your first visit, the place is now a rank wilderness. The lawns have become a waterlogged marsh dotted with fungi. Insects skirl above stagnant ponds and dense weeds have choked the life from the trees. A creeping miasma cloaks out the sunlight.

A single breath of this foul air is enough to slay your men. You'll die yourself unless you have a blessing of Immunity to Disease/Poison. (If you did have such a blessing, remember to cross it off now it's used up.)

If, thanks to a blessing, you survived, turn to **64**. Otherwise turn to **123**.

434

You pass a group of miners on their way back to the surface. They are bony sallow-faced wretches clad in rags. The well-to-do lords who own this mine pay their workers barely more than they need to stay alive.

If you have the codeword *Church*, turn to **453**. If not, turn to **471**.

435

The pirates seize you and clap you in iron fetters, then put your own vessel in tow and start the long haul back to their base.

Cross off your money and possessions, along with any Cargo Units aboard your vessel. However, do not cross the ship and crew off your Ship's Manifest just yet. You may still be able to escape from your captors…

Turn to **454**.

436

You must fend for yourself, surviving on little more than wild berries and cold spring water while you scour the bleak hills. Make a SCOUTING roll at a Difficulty of 14.

Successful SCOUTING roll	turn to **546**
Failed SCOUTING roll	turn to **601**

437

A pack of hellions erupt out of the sea by night and pelt your vessel with burning pitch. To repulse them you must use a combination of sorcery and holy force. Make MAGIC and SANCTITY rolls, both at Difficulty 17.

Both rolls successful	The hellions retreat; turn to **322**
One roll successful	The ship's aflame; turn to **249**
Both rolls failed	Carried off to hell; turn to **66** in *Into the Underworld*

438

You arrive at the coast to see your own ship riding at anchor. A gang of pirates armed with whips are forcing your own sailors to equip her as a war vessel. Your blood boils at the thought of the Reavers using your ship for their own ends.

Charge in to rescue your men	turn to **603**
Reconnoitre the island first	turn to **655**

439

Along with your crew, you cower below decks with your hands over your ears. The ship drifts on untended with no one but Fate at the tiller, and slowly that deathly singing fades into the distance. Roll two dice.

Score 2-6	The ship hits a reef	turn to **486**
Score 7+	Adrift in unknown waters	turn to **244**

440

You take 250 Shards from her money pouch. It is little enough compensation for all she's put you through in the past. Hearing her moan and turn over in her sleep, you give her the empty money pouch to cuddle. What a grand joke, when the swashbuckling burglar wakes to find she's been robbed!

You quietly let yourself out, pleased to have settled the score after so long. Lose the codeword *Anger* and turn to **675**.

441

Earlier in the day you had to order a lashing for one of the crew because of insubordination. Having escaped from the brig, the wretch comes stealing in on you in the night. If not for a creaky floorboard he would have cut your throat while you slept. As it is, he gets first blow and you must fight him without the benefit of weapon or armour.

Resentful Sailor, COMBAT 5, Defence 6, Stamina 3

If you manage to overcome him, turn to **262**.

442

'It is the god Jiarosh, who dwells inside the mountain!' shriek the islanders as plumes of thick black smoke start to boil out of the volcano's cone. 'Jiarosh, spare us!'

Evacuate the island	turn to **384**
Intercede with the god	turn to **404**
Set sail at once	turn to **479**

443

It is Targdaz, your personal sorcerer.

'Still gallivanting about on the high seas?' he says. 'There are much more interesting things afoot back home. I'm on my way there now. Want a ride?'

'What about the ship?'

'I'm sure these fellows are capable of sailing it to port without you
to tell them what to do.'

    Fly off on Targdaz's horse   turn to **405**

    Decline his offer   turn to **135**

444

Jiarosh, the vulcanian god of the island, regards your entreaties as gross
impertinence. He sends forth a spurt of lava and deadly hot gas that
incinerates you where you stand. Turn to **123**.

445

These tunnels connect places from all corners of the world. You soon
get your bearings. From here you can travel where you wish, emerging
by magic through a vent in empty space.

To Aku	*The Court of Hidden Faces* **444**
To Brazen	turn to **99**
To Chambara	*Lords of the Rising Sun* **79**
To Dangor	*The City in the Clouds* **3**
To Dunpala	*The Serpent King's Domain* **42**
To Dweomer	turn to **571**
To Mithdrak	*The Isle of a Thousand Spires* **50**
To Pethumar	*The Lone and Level Sands* **20**
To Ringhorn	*Cities of Gold and Glory* **2**
To Smogmaw	turn to **44**
To Teleos	*Legions of the Labyrinth* **88**
To Yarimura	*The Plains of Howling Darkness* **10**
To Yellowport	*The War-Torn Kingdom* **10**

446

The men are horrified at your callousness. 'I thank the gods it wasn't me
who fell overboard,' growls the first mate in a surly fashion.

    'You should say: "it was not I",' you point out.

    Correcting his grammar only puts him into a darker mood. For the
next couple of days, neither he nor anyone else will so much as
acknowledge your presence.

    Turn to **677**.

447

If you have the title Chosen One of Nagil, turn to **466**. If not, turn to **484**.

448

One of the sailors comes over drenched in blood and hands you a trophy that he hacked from one of the creatures' maws. It is a **hydra's tooth**. Note it on your list of possessions before turning to **118**.

449

You realize that it is too risky to linger here. You scale the cliffs under cover of darkness and find a beach on the far side of the island, where you can make your camp at a safe distance from the cursed village.

Turn to **177**.

450

A low prow emerges from a bank of mist close off your starboard bow. As the vessel takes shape, you recognize the bronze shields along the sides that identify it as a slave ship from Uttaku. It heaves ponderously closer – powered, not by sails, but by huge paddles turned by oxen chained in the bowels of the ship.

'Normally we could hope to outrun them,' announces the helmsman. 'But they've come on us right close, and there's hardly a breath of wind for the sails. We'll have to stand and fight.'

The crew awaits your orders.

Go alongside and prepare to board	turn to **523**
Ram the Uttakin ship	turn to **541**

451

You know that the snakes will detect your approach even in darkness, because they can sense your body heat. To counteract this you take a long dip in the ocean until you are shivering with cold. Then you return to slay the Gorgons in their sleep…

Make a THIEVERY roll at a Difficulty of 10.

Successful THIEVERY roll	turn to **487**
Failed THIEVERY roll	turn to **506**

To one side of the tunnel is a shaft that has been boarded up. On it is stuck a label which reads: 'Danger. This section of the mines closed on account of spectres. By order of the Mine Supervisor.'

Break down the boards   turn to **470**
Venture deeper   turn to **651**
Head for the surface   turn to **25**

Among the shambling miners you notice one face – your former helmsman, Gaspar Savaloy. His cheeks, once ruddy and well-larded as any yeoman of Golnir, are now hollow; his formerly ample belly has been lost along with memories of good meals.

'Mister Savaloy,' you say. 'Here's a pretty pass, eh?'

It takes a few seconds for recognition to strike. 'Skipper! If it ain't me old skipper what I unjustly abandoned on that isle.' He starts to sway his head, eyes too parched for tears. 'Help yer old helmsman, skipper.'

You discover from the mine supervisor that it will cost 30 Shards to pay off Savaloy's indenture.

| Pay to have him freed | turn to **489** |
| Ignore him and walk on | turn to **471** |

454

Get the codeword *Colour* and turn to **472**.

455

The tavern is a shambles. Several of your men lie dead in the wreckage. The first mate staggers over and you are horrified to see that one of his eyes has been gouged out in the fighting.

'Yeah, but you should see the other bloke,' he quips gamely.

You have the chance to gain a Rank now. You need to roll higher than your current Rank on one die to do so. If you do go up a Rank, permanently increase your Stamina by 1-6 points (the score of one die) and remember that your Defence score will increase by 1.

Your men are in no shape to tackle the Reavers now. 'He who fights and runs away, skipper…' urges the bosun.

You nod in agreement. 'Get back aboard, you swabs. We're setting sail!'

Turn to **164**.

456

The pirates pull alongside and cast grappling hooks to seize your vessel. Within moments they are swarming aboard. You offer them your goods, but plead for the freedom of your crew. Make a CHARISMA roll at a Difficulty of 15.

| Successful CHARISMA roll | turn to **416** |
| Failed CHARISMA roll | turn to **435** |

457

Lose 1-6 Stamina points. If you survive, you lead your men in a charge that routs the remaining pirates. Searching the bodies of those you killed, you can help yourself to a **sword (COMBAT +2)** and a suit of **chain mail (Defence +3)**.

'We ought to get under way,' says the first mate. 'They'll be back with reinforcements soon.'

You agree. Lose the codeword *Colour* and turn to **164**.

458

The Reavers have no intention of releasing your ship and crew; slave labour is too valuable.

If you have a **silver medallion**, turn to **567**. If not, you must decide whether to sneak off and rescue your men (turn to **438**) or forget about them and see to your own future (turn to **476**).

459

Lauria is sleeping like an innocent babe. She barely murmurs in her sleep as you toss her over your shoulder and carry her down to the docks. There you find an Uttakin slaver who is delighted to buy her off you for 150 Shards. 'She has very white skin,' he says appreciatively.

You nod. 'And a black heart.'

Lose the codeword *Anger* and get the codeword *Civil* in its place. Then turn to **100**.

460

The lookout reports seeing a meteor plunge out of the sky a few leagues to southward. The first mate thinks it might be worth investigating, but it is not as easy as he thinks. You will have to calculate how far the ship has gone since the meteor fell and then plot a course back. This requires a SCOUTING roll at a Difficulty of 16.

Successful SCOUTING roll	turn to **409**
Failed SCOUTING roll	turn to **262**

461

The fertile slopes of the volcano are covered with lush vegetation. The islanders are pleased to gather round and offer you a feast of fried yams, shellfish stew, barbecued fowl and beer made from pineapple juice.

Roll two dice.

Score 2-6	The volcano starts to rumble	turn to **442**
Score 7-12	The volcano remains dormant	turn to **706**

462

It is the wizard Targdaz, whom you freed from imprisonment inside a giant ruby. 'I have come to tell you of a vacant castle in Old Harkuna,' he says. 'If you'd care to take up residence there I'd be happy to serve as your court sorcerer.'

`Fine, but where is it exactly?'

He throws up his hands. `I didn't bring a map! It can't be that hard to find.'

So saying, he flies off. Turn to **135**.

463

You believe that everything points to the bosun as the man responsible for this heinous crime. You order him clapped in irons, but the crew protest that he is a man of unblemished character who would never kill anyone except in an honest brawl.

Press the matter	turn to **677**
Let it drop	turn to **554**

464

You walk down into pitch darkness. The scent is of damp loam and ozone. Sorcery is in the very air here, strong enough to make your skin tingle. To master the winding paths below the world you must make a MAGIC or SCOUTING roll (your choice) at a Difficulty of 17.

Successful roll	turn to **445**
Failed roll	*Into the Underworld* **25**

465

You are gazing over the side when you see a dark shadow rising from the depths. It is huge.

Before you have a chance to shout any warning, colossal tentacles rear up from the water and grapple the ship.

Roll one die if your ship is a barque, two dice if she's a brigantine, and three dice if she's a galleon. You can add your Rank to this roll.

Score 2-9	The ship is lost	turn to **592**
Score 10-15	You escape in the cutter	turn to **610**
Score 16+	The Kraken departs	turn to **135**

466 ☐

The skeletons have sailed from the Night Country to pay homage to you. Your men are astonished to see them kneel down in your cabin and bow their bald white heads, as docile as page-boys.

If the box above is empty, put a tick in it and turn to **502**. If the box was ticked already, turn to **521**.

467

You kneel at the end of the headland and concentrate on your prayers. Towards dusk, with the sun a pulsing globe of orange fire on the horizon, you hear a footstep on the rocks behind you. Make a SANCTITY roll at a Difficulty of 12.

Successful SANCTITY roll	turn to **485**
Failed SANCTITY roll	turn to **121**

468

You reach the coastal waters of the Sleeping Isle.

'We're going to have to find anchorage here,' says the first mate when you ask for his report. 'We're in need of fresh supplies and the ship could do with light repairs.'

You drop anchor in a bay fringed by coconut palms and go ashore in the rowboat. While the men gather supplies, you have the opportunity to explore a little way inland if you wish.

Explore the island	turn to **265**
Help gather supplies	turn to **284**

469

You lower yourself to the floor and pad softly over to where the two Gorgons lie sleeping. In that sleep of dreams what death may come... if only you are stealthy enough. Make a THIEVERY roll at a Difficulty of 15.

Successful THIEVERY roll	turn to **487**
Failed THIEVERY roll	turn to **506**

470 ☐

If the box above is empty, put a tick in it and turn to **488**. If it was already ticked, turn to **507**.

471

No daylight penetrates this far below ground. To proceed you must have a **candle**, **lantern** or other source of light. Otherwise you have no choice but to turn back.

Proceed downwards	turn to **509**
Head for the surface	turn to **317**

472

You are chained by the pirates and taken inland on one of the Unnumbered Isles. The landscape consists of windswept bluffs under a sky of perpetual racing clouds. A thin cold drizzle comes down in gusts.

Get the codeword *Chance* if you can succeed in a SCOUTING check at Difficulty 12. Whether you make the roll or not, turn to **114**.

473

The new Reaver King, Isthmus Jack, is a strutting rogue with a broad bald brow and a beard like shavings of red gold. He has none of Amcha's cold intensity, but behind that cavalier grin you get a feeling of simmering menace.

'Ah,' he says, 'you slew my predecessor, I believe?'

Admit to killing Amcha	turn to **512**
Deny it	turn to **400**

474

The pirates ram you, then pour across the rail brandishing their swords. This promises to be a hard fight.

Roll three dice if you are a Warrior, or two dice if you belong to any other profession. Add your Rank to this roll. Then, if your crew is poor quality, subtract 2 from the total. If the crew is good quality, add 2. If the crew is excellent quality, add 3.

Score 0-4	Calamity; you are killed	turn to **123**
Score 5-9	Crushing defeat; lose 2-12 Stamina	turn to **435**
Score 10-13	Forced to give in; lose 1-6 Stamina	turn to **416**
Score 14-17	The pirates withdraw	turn to **13**
Score 18+	Outright victory	turn to **492**

475

You are off the coast of Old Harkuna with the Sorcerers' Isle not many leagues to the south east.

Steer north	*The Court of Hidden Faces* **60**
Steer south	turn to **208**
Steer east	turn to **200**
Steer west	turn to **21**
Make for Ringhorn	*The Court of Hidden Faces* **26**
Head for Dweomer	turn to **9**

476

You're obliged to fall in with the Reavers, at least for a while. You are given a midshipman's position aboard one of their vessels and told that promotion will depend on how you acquit yourself in this job.

Make a THIEVERY roll and a SCOUTING roll, both at Difficulty 14.

Both rolls successful	turn to **494**
One roll successful	turn to **513**
Fail both rolls	turn to **531**

477 ☐

If the box is empty, put a tick in it and turn to **622**. If it was already ticked, turn to **675**.

478

A gust of wind swings the boom around, knocking the ship's surgeon into the sea. Like most sailors, who prefer the thought of a quick death if their ships should go down, he cannot swim. The men crowd along the rail, watching helplessly as he founders in the water.

Jump in to save the surgeon	turn to **558**
Leave him to drown	turn to **446**
Order the helmsman to put about	turn to **360**

479

You sail away from the Island of Fire. The first mate comes to your cabin to discuss the course you wish to steer.

Go north	turn to **246**
Go south	turn to **192**

Go east   turn to **210**
Go west   turn to **303**

480

A flotilla of mossy pontoons come drifting across the water towards you. They look like floating gardens. As they get closer you can see people and animals moving between brightly coloured tents on each pontoon. They are the sea gypsies, who live on these large clumps of floating weeds.

As soon as they draw alongside, the gypsies clamber aboard without waiting for permission and start shoving a curious assortment of goods towards you.

'Best prices on the high seas!' says one with a cavalier grin.

Item	To buy	To sell
Rope	30 Shards	20 Shards
Lantern	75 Shards	60 Shards
Candle	10 Shards	5 Shards
Water flask	25 Shards	20 Shards
Coral-red tresses	1000 Shards	500 Shards
Golden katana	10000 Shards	3000 Shards
Smoulder fish	110 Shards	90 Shards
Cross-staff (SCOUTING +2)	700 Shards	500 Shards
Violin	90 Shards	50 Shards
Parrot	200 Shards	90 Shards
Fishing hook	5 Shards	2 Shards
Boar's tusk	150 Shards	75 Shards
Green gem	575 Shards	100 Shards

When you have finished your buying and selling, turn to **50**.

481

You give each man a biscuit from the cabin boy's locker and tell him to swallow it. One of the ordinary seamen, a hulking fellow called Timung, is unable to do so. Guilt has left his mouth too dry.

Later, a gold chain that belonged to the victim is found under Timung's pillow, showing that his motive was simple theft. You have no compunction about casting the villain overboard to try his luck in battle with the sharks.

Roll two dice, and if you get higher than your current THIEVERY score, increase it by 1. Then turn to **188**.

482

'Few reach this far,' booms a voice. Startled, you whirl around and peer in all directions, but there is nothing to be seen except the pall of leaves and trees like silent sentinels.

The branches of the plane tree move – sluggish serpents stirred to drowsy life, unfolding to reveal a fissure in the earth.

`Where does it lead?' you ask the unseen presence.

`Anywhere you wish, if you have the science to find your way. But to the unskilled it is only a gateway to hell.'

Enter the hole   turn to **464**

Turn back   turn to **388**

483

At dawn you find you are in the Misty Estuary. The helmsman is at a loss to explain it. `I could have sworn we were a hundred leagues north of here,' he says.

You are not one to ignore the suggestions of providence. Since some force has seen fit to bring you here, it may be worth staying a while.

Note that your ship is now docked at Smogmaw and then turn to **44**.

484

Clutched in bony fingers, you and your men are hauled across to the other ship. Shrouds catch a foetid wind and slowly she picks up speed, leaving your own ship to drift abandoned.

You are pressed into service below decks – a harsh servitude from which not even death can bring deliverance. Each day you watch with horror as your flesh dries up and sloughs away, leaving you a macabre living skeleton.

Nothing can save you from undeath – not even any resurrection you may have arranged. Cross off all codewords and ticks in all your Fabled Lands books and start again with a new character.

485

You are dazzled from staring so long in the direction of the setting sun, so that all you can see when you turn is the silhouettes of the two tall women who have come to confront you. Their hair seems to move – not lightly, as though whipped by the sea breeze, but with the oily sluggishness of snakes.

Attack them	turn to **685**
Freeze	turn to **356**
Retreat	turn to **374**

486

The ship keels over; timbers warp and split; mere anarchy is loosed upon you. Seawater rushes into the broken shell of the hull drowning out the cries of your crewmen. Cross them and the ship off your Ship's Manifest. You can think of nothing now but saving yourself.

Roll two dice. If the score is greater than your Rank, you are drowned (turn to **123**). If the score is less than or equal to your Rank, you are swept miraculously towards a shore of white coral sand. Lose 2-12 Stamina points and (if you can survive that) turn to **505**.

487

Near their bedside is a **dagger** which you can add to your list of possessions if you wish. Whether you keep it or not, it is a handy tool with which to do your night's business. The Gorgons' necks are tough and fibrous with almost no blood, and once the heads are hacked off the serpentine coiffure wilts like a torn-up weed.

Turn to **393**.

488

The weight of the air above becomes almost palpable as you descend deep into the ground. A trickle of sweat runs down your spine. Each breath you take tastes hot and stale.

Turning a bend in the passage, you see a sight to harrow your soul. Wreathed in silver light, a group of frightful-visaged spectres are turning slowly in the air, dancing a slow minuet to the mournful tune of an invisible harpsichord.

Use a **spectral veil** (if you have one)   turn to **525**

Banish them with holy words   turn to **543**
Leave before they see you   turn to **561**

489

You go back to the mine office and sign the necessary papers. Cross off 30 Shards.

Gaspar Savaloy falls on his knees to thank you. You look down in a mixture of contempt and pity as he kisses your boots.

'A tidy reward for mutiny, wouldn't you say, Mister Savaloy?'

He cannot look you in the eye. 'I'm shamed, skipper; you've shamed me. But I'll make up all I owe you an' more, you see if I don't. I'm bound for Dweomer, where I'll make good. Then I can pay you back.'

He scurries off. Get the codeword *Cancel* and turn to **317**.

490

You hail the other ship, asking its crew why they serve a monarch who is long dead.

'Not dead but sleeping,' counters the captain. 'We are the keepers of the flame until that time when the Rimewater thaws and our liege-lord shall rise up to sweep the Uttakin into the sea.'

Your first mate leans over and whispers in your ear. 'Fanatics, by the sound of it, captain.'

You shrug. 'Who knows?'

The royalist ship sails off. Turn to **475**.

491

It is as though night has fallen suddenly in the middle of the day. Thunderheads hunch on the horizon like vast brooding crows. Lightning streaks yellow fire across the tortured sky.

'Doomsday!' shrieks the bosun. 'Repent or be damned!'

If you have the blessing of Alvir and Valmir, which confers Safety from Storms, you can ignore the storm. Cross off your blessing and turn to **24**.

If you have no blessing, the storm hits with full force. Rain rattles against the juddering canvas; waves lash the deck. Roll one die if your ship is a barque, two dice if it is a brigantine, or three dice if it is a galleon. Add 1 to the roll if you have an excellent quality crew; subtract

1 if you have a poor quality crew.

Score 0-4	Your ship sinks	turn to **157**
Score 5-6	The mast splits	turn to **670**
Score 7-19	You weather the storm	turn to **42**

492

The pirates' treasure amounts to 600 Shards. Record it on your Adventure Sheet. Their ship's hold contains 1 Cargo Unit of metals, which you can add to your own cargo if you have room for it. The mate advises you take the **pirate captain's head**, which may bring a reward.

It was your leadership that won the day. Roll two dice, and if the result is greater than your current Rank then you gain a Rank. You also gain 1-6 Stamina points permanently: increase your normal (unwounded) Stamina score by the roll of one die. Remember that going up in Rank increases your Defence.

Once you have made the necessary adjustments to your Adventure Sheet, turn to **13**.

493

The pirates do not stand on ceremony. You are hauled out on to the high terrace of the citadel and impaled on an iron spike. Your body will hang there, staring sightlessly out to sea, until the carrion birds have eaten their fill.

Lose the codewords *Colour* and *Crocus* if you had them, and then turn to **123**.

494 ☐

If the box above is empty, put a tick in it and turn to **621**. If the box was already ticked, turn to **639**.

495

If your ship is docked here you can put to sea. If not, you could pay for passage to either Dweomer or Metriciens, at a cost of 35 Shards in each case, or to Smogmaw for 15 Shards.

Put to sea	turn to **19**
Pay for passage to Smogmaw	turn to **535**
Pay for passage to Dweomer	turn to **242**

Pay for passage to Metriciens   turn to **260**

496

The horse, a magnificent white stallion with a mane of silver threads, drops rapidly out of the sky to alight gently on the deck.

If you have the codeword *Dragon*, turn to **462**. If not but you have the codeword *Edifice*, turn to **443**. If you have neither codeword, turn to **424**.

497

The mountain turns out to be a hollow rocky shell with steps winding down inside it. You stand at the top and gaze down the deep shaft. A faint sulphurous tang rises on the wind from far below.

Descend the steps	*Into the Underworld* **5**
Return down the mountainside	turn to **606**

498

A blessing costs 20 Shards if you are an initiate, 40 Shards otherwise. You cannot buy a blessing from Molhern if you already have one.

Molhern's blessing allows you a second attempt at any one failed MAGIC roll. After the second roll (whether successful or not) the blessing is used up.

If you buy a blessing, write: MAGIC reroll (one use) in the Blessings box on your Adventure Sheet.

Now turn to **99**.

499

There is an old adage: set a thief to catch a thief. Presumably, with a little leeway, the same principle should mean that any crafty rogue can spot the loopholes in a villain's alibi.

Make a THIEVERY roll at a Difficulty of 14.

Successful THIEVERY roll	turn to **481**
Failed THIEVERY roll	turn to **463**

500

The **witch's hand** casts a spell, animating the head so that it flies from your belt and tries to snap your throat between its teeth.

You must fight the grisly thing.

Head, COMBAT 7, Defence 14, Stamina 5

You cannot flee. If you win, cross the **pirate captain's head** off your list of possessions and turn to **482**.

501

You don't even bother to look round when you hear the lookout call, 'Flying fish!'

A moment later you are hit in the back by a shark that has soared out of the sea on wide fins. Other flying sharks are attacking your crew, who are joining up to deal with them. But you are alone on the poopdeck, and must fight your shark unaided.

Flying shark, COMBAT 9, Defence 10, Stamina 27

If you manage to kill it, turn to **320**.

502

The jaw of the skeletal captain drops open and a chilling voice issues forth: 'Go to Chompo in Akatsurai. There you will find a clue that will lead you to the tomb of the necromancer Dawatsu Morituri, whom you must set free. This is our dread lord's command.'

They return to their vessel and sail off. Get the codeword *Cenotaph* and then turn to **321**.

503

The shrine consists of nothing more than an obelisk of smooth green stone raised on a sandbank out in the estuary. The priest tells you that to gain a blessing you must swim out to the obelisk. To succeed in this you must make a SCOUTING roll at a Difficulty of 11.

Successful SCOUTING roll	turn to **147**
Failed SCOUTING roll	turn to **165**
Don't make the attempt	turn to **44**

504

You sail into the stretch of ocean known as the Sea of Reeds, which lies between Braelak and the Unnumbered Isles.

Roll two dice.

Score 2-3	Storm	turn to **598**

Score 4-6	A gypsy caravan?	turn to **480**
Score 7-8	An uneventful voyage	turn to **50**
Score 9-12	A bank of reeds	turn to **516**

505

You are on a stretch of shore. Surf pounds on white sand. At the back of the beach is a wall of craggy grey rocks covered with hanging ferns. It is the classic desert island.

Turn to **177**.

506

You step softly across the cavern floor. A hiss and spit makes you jump and look over your shoulder, but it is only a damp log gleaming sullenly in the embers of the hearth.

You look back at the beds. With a thrill of alarm you see they are now empty.

Turn to **121**.

507

You descend into a small chamber where some boxes are stacked up. Four men who are playing cards by the light of an oil lamp turn to you with startled looks. Before you can say a word, they have drawn cudgels from inside their jerkins and are advancing to do business.

Make a COMBAT roll at a Difficulty of 13.

| Successful COMBAT roll | turn to **579** |
| Failed COMBAT roll | turn to **597** |

508

You are wandering through the picturesque cobbled streets of old Dweomer. The place lies under a perpetual shroud of drizzle, except when thick fog billows in off the sea each morning. Narrow latticed windows give glimpses of warm drawing-rooms inside the colleges.

If you have the codeword *Cancel*, turn to **526**. If not, turn to **687**.

509 ☐

You continue down the shaft until you reach the rock face, where there are several wheelbarrows stacked with copper ore. No one is working here at the moment, but the next shift will arrive soon.

If the box on the preceding page is empty, put a tick in it and turn to **377**. If it was already ticked, turn to **396**.

510

Get the codeword *Colour*.

People come flocking down from the citadel to watch you sail into the bay. There are hundreds of them — not just the crews of the pirate vessels, but their wives and children too. This is a complete community, just like any number of other towns around the world except that their livelihood rests on bare-faced villainy.

To impress on them that you are not to be trifled with you must make a CHARISMA roll at Difficulty 15. (You can add 2 to the dice roll if your ship is a galleon, and 1 if you have an excellent crew.)

Successful CHARISMA roll	turn to **656**
Failed CHARISMA roll	turn to **114**

511

'A pirate galley!' cries the lookout. You follow the direction he's pointing to see a ship flying the red pennant of the Kingdom of the Reavers. Her oars give her a good burst of speed over short distances, and she is soon bearing down on you.

Make a run for it   turn to **529**

Parley   turn to **547**
Fight it out   turn to **565**

512

Your answer seems to put Isthmus Jack in a good mood. He bellows with vicious laughter and tells several stories that portray the old king, Amcha One-Eye, in a bad light.

Suddenly he stops laughing and gives you a long hard stare. It is at this moment that you realize he's quite insane.

If you have a **pirate captain's head**, turn to **638**. Otherwise, turn to **656**.

513

You rise to the rank of second mate, but a couple of close shaves with the Sokaran navy convince you to get out while the going's good.

You jump ship in Smogmaw after first helping yourself to a **sword (COMBAT +1)** from the ship's magazine.

Turn to **44**.

514

Lauria wakes up and launches herself across the darkened bedroom with a blood-curdling yell. In the faint stray beam of a street lamp you see a glint of metal in her hand.

Make a COMBAT roll at a Difficulty of 13.

Successful COMBAT roll   turn to **532**
Failed COMBAT roll   turn to **550**

515 ☐

You come across a man crouching miserably on a desolate reef. 'If you had not come along I would have been dead before the end of the week,' he says tearfully as you help him aboard.

If the box above is empty, put a tick in it and turn to **608**. If the box was already ticked, turn to **572**.

516

'Curse the luck!' snarls the helmsman. 'We're caught in these reeds.'

You look over the side. Thick fronds of drifting weed snag your rudder and choke the water in all directions. Roll one die.

Score 1-2	Drift with the current	turn to **534**
Score 3-4	Sea gypsies arrive	turn to **552**
Score 5	Becalmed	turn to **570**
Score 6	You break free	turn to **50**

517

You while away several hours chatting to the priest. He is a simple man of peasant stock, rather superstitious but easy to get on with. He tells you all sorts of fables he has heard – some of them containing a grain of truth, no doubt.

Among the stories he tells you are accounts of Starspike Island, which he claims has a mountain so high that no one can breathe at its summit, of the Island of Fire, which he believes to be an active volcano, and the Sleeping Isle, where a spell puts all who arrive there into deep slumber.

It is time you were on your way. 'Do you need a blessing?' asks the priest. Turn to **498**.

518

Days pass and the supplies are running low when finally you see another vessel sailing towards you. She is an Akatsuran slave ship bound for the Black Pagoda. Her master is reluctant to approach because of the plague, but at last you prevail on him to put aboard a few of his slaves who are too frail or intractable to be worth transporting further.

As the Akatsuran ship sails off, your motley handful of new crewmen raise three cheers. 'You've saved us from a pretty dire fate, skipper,' says a fellow who appoints himself your first mate. 'We'll do our best to serve you faithfully.'

Note that your Crew Quality is now poor and turn to **337**.

519

The Akatsurese captain is grateful for everything you've told him. 'Now I can get a good deal on my cargo,' he says.

He presents you with a **golden katana (COMBAT +1)** and tells you that you will be welcome in the city of Chambara.

Returning to your own ship, you sail on. Turn to **228**.

520

The men say nothing, only look at you reproachfully as you get into the cutter and row away from the becalmed ship.

'If looks were curses,' the first mate says in your ear, 'we'd fry in hell tonight.'

Cross the vessel's details off your Ship's Manifest. After days at sea the others have succumbed to thirst and fever. You are left to bend doggedly over the oars, determined to struggle for life until the gods see fit to snuff out your wretched life.

At last you see a stretch of shoreline. You shake the mate's arm, trying to rouse him, but he is stiff and cold. The others too – all are dead. You alone survive to stagger ashore.

Turn to **313**.

521

The skeletons present you with tribute in the form of antique coins and jewellery from the lockers of sunken wrecks. The total value of this haul is 750 Shards.

'Till death do us join,' calls out the skeletal captain as he sails away. Turn to **321**.

522

You cannot break free of the Gorgons' curse. You are doomed to remain stock-still, a living statue, until worn down by time and wind and rain. Erase all codewords, ticks and notes on your Adventure Sheet and start again (at 1 in any Fabled Lands book) with a new character.

523

You cast grappling hooks to hold your vessel alongside the slavers' ship while ladders are flung out to allow your crew to go aboard. The Uttakin warriors stand ready to receive you; their smiles give a sensation of grim foreboding.

Roll three dice if you are a Warrior, or two dice if you belong to any other profession. Add your Rank to this roll.

Then, if your crew is poor quality, subtract 2 from the total. If the crew is good quality, add 2. If the crew is excellent quality, add 3.

Score 0-4   You are killed   turn to **123**

Score 5-15	Enslaved; lose 2-12 Stamina	turn to **613**
Score 16-17	The Uttakin withdraw	turn to **300**
Score 18+	Outright victory	turn to **559**

524

You are woken by a sound in the night. Your heart is pounding and you are soaked in sweat. You must have been having a nightmare. Either that or you know what is to come. Turn to **121**.

525

The spectres mistake you for one of their own kind. They converse with you on such subjects as the vapours of the moon, the quality of the afterlife, and the true nature of eternity. These are secrets that no mortal ever heard, and you will never be the same again.

Gain one Rank. You can permanently increase your unwounded Stamina score by 1-6 points (the roll of one die). Also, going up in Rank will increase your Defence by 1. Turn to **633**.

526

You run into old Gaspar Savaloy, who was once your helmsman. He has filled out to his former rotund figure since the time you rescued him from virtual slavery in the mines on Copper Island. His clothes are quite fine too – as befits a man who is now one of the wealthiest merchants in these parts.

`Care to speculate, skipper?' he asks you. `I've got a hot tip that's sure to show a profit.'

Make an investment	turn to **652**
Check on an earlier investment	turn to **359**
Bid him good-day	turn to **687**

527

`Er, something for your cellar, Master,' you say lamely, handing over the **bottle of wine**. (Cross it off your Adventure Sheet.)

`Splendid,' says the Master, somewhat mollified. `And rest assured that I've been keeping abreast of your work... er, whatever your name is... and I think you can expect good marks at the end of term. Mantel will show you out.' Turn to **607**.

528

You wait until midnight before setting off on foot. You are alone. Your men didn't sign up to fight as marines in a nocturnal raid, and in any case it will be easier to sneak into the pirate camp on your own. Get the codeword *Crocus* and turn to **362**.

529

Roll two dice and add your Rank. Add 1 to the total if you have an average crew, 2 if you have a good crew, or 3 if you have an excellent crew.

Score 1-6	The pirates overtake you	turn to **565**
Score 7+	You outrun them	turn to **32**

530

You find a ship drifting on the open sea. Her sails are furled, fluttering gently in the breeze.

'I can't see anyone aboard, captain,' hollers the lookout.

Go alongside	turn to **548**
Sail past	turn to **32**

531

Your short and inglorious career as a pirate is cut short when you are left behind after a disastrous attack on an Uttakin merchantman. You are hung from the yardarm with minimal fuss and the sailors do not even bother to watch you 'kicking Nagil's jig' as the expression goes. Turn to **123**.

532

You lay Lauria out with a right cross. She'll wake up with a bad headache, but that was on the cards anyway after the amount of cider she drank. You take the opportunity to steal 250 Shards and a **dagger (COMBAT +1)** before sneaking off into the night. Lose the codeword *Anger* and turn to **675**.

533

Wavering like will-o'-the-wisps above a light haze, a ship's lights gradually appear out of the night. A pallid mariner in a ragged, ancient-looking coat calls to you from the rail, saying that the ship is under a curse. Behind him stand a throng of sad-faced seamen.

'We cannot put in to any port,' the captain explains in a hollow voice, 'but are doomed to sail the high seas forevermore.'

If you want to lift the curse you will need to make a MAGIC roll at a Difficulty of 15.

Lift the curse   turn to **410**

Fail (or don't try)   turn to **137**

534

It takes several days to clean off all the reeds that were clogging the rudder.

Roll one die to see where the current has taken you.

Score 1	turn to **301**
Score 2	turn to **205**
Score 3	turn to **42**
Score 4	turn to **281**
Score 5	turn to **402**
Score 6	turn to **189**

535

Fair winds and calm seas bring you swiftly to the southern continent. You sail up the Nozama River, which is so wide at this point that the far bank is barely visible as a thin line of muddy green under a sun-washed sky.

The captain points to a shanty town on the near bank. Behind it, the jungle broods under a haze of steam. 'Smogmaw,' he says.

Cross off the 15 Shards for your voyage if you haven't paid already, then turn to **44**.

536

The accused protests his innocence, but you are convinced he is guilty. As he is tossed overboard he shrieks a curse on everyone aboard. Only later do you find out he was the seventh son of a seventh son, born in Dweomer during an eclipse of the moon.

To deflect the curse you must make a MAGIC roll at Difficulty 14.

Successful MAGIC roll	turn to **188**
Failed MAGIC roll	turn to **641**

537

You reach a clearing where a vast blue plane tree stands, its branches twisted chaotically, some stretching towards the sky, others resting like tired serpents on the ground. There is a feeling of being watched by hundreds of invisible eyes.

If you possess a **pirate captain's head**, turn to **500**. If not, turn to **482**.

538

You encounter a ship bound from Dangor, where the harbour is set in cliffs a thousand feet above the sea and vessels must be winched up. The captain hails you and says he has a Cargo Unit of minerals in his hold that he would be willing to exchange for one Cargo Unit of any other commodity.

Alter the details on your Ship's Manifest if you trade cargoes with him, then turn to **3**.

539

The skeletons are all around you. They make a noise like the rattling of hollow sticks as they clasp your limbs and try to bear you to the cabin floor.

To drive them off you must make a COMBAT roll at a Difficulty of 15.

Successful COMBAT roll	turn to **557**
Failed COMBAT roll	turn to **484**

540

On the way up the cliff path you pass a few seagulls that stand dead still, no doubt under the same spell that afflicts the villagers. Ahead lies a great bronze door set in the rocks. You have a feeling that is where you'll find the source of the trouble.

Knock boldly on the door	turn to **631**
Look for a way to sneak in	turn to **649**

541

Roll two dice and add your Rank. Add 1 to the total if you have an average crew, 2 if you have a good crew, or 3 if you have an excellent crew.

Score 1-6	Boarding action	turn to **523**
Score 7-10	Enemy ship crippled	turn to **577**
Score 11+	Enemy ship sinks	turn to **595**

542

You discover that *Walks in the Forest of Larun*, by Bosquay d'Arborealle, is missing from the shelves. When you point this out to the librarian he looks in his files and says, 'Ah yes, that book is out on loan to the Master of the College. It's overdue, actually.'

'You should tell him to return it.'

He gives you an extraordinary look. 'You tell him!'

Turn to **368**.

543

You step forward into the ghost-light. The spectres fall silent and turn like drifting wisps of smoke to face you. 'What's this?' you cry in outrage. 'If tombs and charnel-houses cannot hold the dead, burials should be made in ravens' guts instead!'

'Will you mock us, mortal?' creaks a dusty voice.

The spectres reach out with white hands, thinking to take your soul, but you confound them by speaking one of the names of Harkun the Creator-God. The spectres disband into tatters of fading ectoplasm.

They departed so suddenly that they left something on the floor of the cavern: a pattern of sparkling lines made up of tiny ice crystals. You stoop, discovering on closer inspection that the lines mark out the steps of their dance. Intriguing. You practice it yourself – a stately minuet which can be easily executed with both dignity and grace.

Get the codeword *Cruel* and then turn to **633**.

544

The sky turns the colour of burning sulphur and begins to spit lightning like gobbets of hot demons' blood.

If you have the blessing of Alvir and Valmir, which confers Safety from Storms, you can ignore the storm. Cross off your blessing and turn to **311**.

Otherwise you are at the mercy of the storm. Roll one die if your ship is a barque, two dice if it is a brigantine, or three dice if a galleon. Add 1 to the roll if you have an excellent crew; subtract 1 if you have a poor crew.

Score 0-4	Your ship sinks	turn to **634**
Score 5-6	The mast splits	turn to **616**
Score 7-19	You weather the storm	turn to **13**

545

You give the order to trim sail, sculling silently closer to the Reavers' stronghold under cover of darkness. The lookout points to lights twinkling at the back of a wide bay. 'There, cap'n!' he says.

'How do you want to play it?' asks the first mate. 'A frontal assault, or go in sneaky-like?'

Sail straight into the bay	turn to **510**
Drop anchor out beyond the headland	turn to **528**
Make for open ocean	turn to **164**

546

You manage to live quite well off the land, even catching a rabbit which makes quite a fine stew with some mushrooms and berries. Recover 2 Stamina points if injured.

If you have the codeword *Colour*, turn to **438**. If not then you could either try making yourself a boat (turn to **637**) or search for a settlement on the island (turn to **655**).

547

The pirates pull alongside and cast grappling hooks to seize your vessel. Within moments they are swarming aboard. You offer them your goods, but plead for the freedom of your crew. Make a CHARISMA roll at a Difficulty of 15.

Successful CHARISMA roll	turn to **416**
Failed CHARISMA roll	turn to **435**

548

You lead a small boarding party over to the deserted ship. As you go aboard, a black cat strolls out from behind a hatch and watches you warily.

Suddenly your bosun pounces forward and seizes the animal. 'Quick, we've got to throw it overboard!' he says.

Let him jettison the cat	turn to **566**
Tell him to leave it alone	turn to **584**

549

You return to the ship and set sail without delay. Lose the codeword *Crocus* if you had it, then turn to **164**.

550

The knife sinks deep into your shoulder. Lose 2-12 Stamina points (the roll of two dice). You realize at once that the knife was coated with poison, and even a scratch will kill you unless you have a blessing of Immunity to Disease/Poison. (If you use such a blessing, remember to cross it off your Adventure Sheet.)

If you are killed, whether by the knife-wound itself or the poison, turn to **123**. If you survive, turn to **532**.

551

A trick of the light throws red shadows against the western clouds. Squinting into the blaze of dying sunlight, you imagine a scene of battle. An owl flies above phalanxes of troops, guiding them to victory against demons with round shields who seem to emerge out of a great blood-washed lake.

'Daydreaming, skipper?' asks the first mate.

Startled out of your reverie, the spell is broken. Now you see only a line of pink clouds under the gathering curtain of night.

Get the codeword *Cyclops* and turn to **59**.

552

A floating mat of interwoven reeds bearing coloured tents can be seen on the horizon. It is one of the caravans of the sea gypsies. They cross to you in coracles.

'You'll never get those reeds off your hull,' they tell you. 'Grow like wildfire, they do. We'll get you free of them for a hundred Shards; how about it?'

'They might be our best bet,' says the bosun.

Pay them 100 Shards	turn to **50**
Try bartering	turn to **715**
Tell them to go away	turn to **570**

553

Note that your ship is now docked at Copper Island and then turn to **99**.

554

The crew despise you for taking no action. They start to mutter about appointing a new captain and putting you ashore on a deserted island.

Lose 1 from your CHARISMA and, using your new score, make a CHARISMA roll at Difficulty 13.

Successful CHARISMA roll	turn to **188**
Failed CHARISMA roll	turn to **599**

555

The hand suddenly goes rigid, its fingers pointing out a narrow toadstool-lined path you had not noticed before.

Follow the path	turn to **537**
Turn back	turn to **388**

556

One of the crew is revealed as a woman who disguised herself in order to sign aboard. Her deception only comes to light because she is about to give birth. 'I thought he – er, she – was getting rather tubby,' says the ship's surgeon.

'Can you deliver the child?' you ask him.

'You're joking. I can barely set a splint.'

There is nothing for it. You must set a course for the Island of Fire, a volcanic isle which is the nearest place where you might find a competent midwife. Thankfully you reach it before the woman goes into labour. The islanders give you a friendly welcome and their chief's wives take the woman to their hut.

Turn to **461**.

557

The skeletons retreat in disorder to their seaweed-festooned hulk and hoist a ragged web of canvas. Your men watch in silence as they sail away.

You notice that your hands are trembling now that shock has had time to set in. You steady them on the rail and bark orders for the crew to stop gawping and get back to work. They speedily comply, only too happy to forget their encounter with the skeletal pirates.

Turn to **321**.

558

These are choppy seas and the strong current makes swimming difficult. You also have the problem of keeping track of the surgeon over the heavy swell.

To rescue him you must make a SCOUTING roll at a Difficulty of 14. If you fail you will be forced to return to the ship without him.

Successful SCOUTING roll	turn to **427**
Failed SCOUTING roll	turn to **22**

559

The enemy ship's hold is full of slaves, many of whom are wealthy men. You are rewarded with 950 Shards for freeing them.

'What shall we do with the surviving Uttakin, cap'n?' asks the master at arms.

'Leave them to the mercy of their former captives,' you tell him. 'We've bigger fish to fry elsewhere.'

After surviving such a tough scrape you might go up in Rank. Roll two dice, and if the result is greater than your current Rank then you gain a Rank. You also gain 1-6 Stamina points permanently: increase your normal (unwounded) Stamina score by the roll of one die. Remember that going up a Rank increases your Defence by 1.

Once you have made the necessary adjustments to your Adventure Sheet, turn to **300**.

560

The Master waves you to a chair and thrusts a glass of sherry into your hand. He then drones on at great length about all manner of subjects. You wake up suddenly to hear him describing the Forest of Larun: `...which may have been the wizard's tomb found by Silvanus Ent. Doctor Ent's studies suggested the demonic door of the tomb would respond to the password `Rebirth'. Who can say why? Let me tell you my own theory...'

You doze off again. When you wake the next time, you are being carried back to your room by two college servants. `You're lucky, sir,' says one chirpily.

`How's that?' you ask, yawning.

`He literally killed the last one with boredom. Stone dead, like!'

Get the codeword *Crag* and turn to **607**.

561

You sneak back up the tunnel. Make a THIEVERY roll at a Difficulty of 12.

Successful THIEVERY roll	turn to **633**
Failed THIEVERY roll	turn to **669**

562

The sky is the colour of burning sulphur. From behind the clouds comes the growl of thunder. The sailors mutter in fear. `It is the wrath of Elnir,' says the mate. `He summons us to our doom!'

If you have the blessing of Alvir and Valmir, which confers Safety from Storms, you can ignore the storm. Cross off your blessing and turn to **13**.

Otherwise the storm hits with undiluted fury. Roll one die if your ship is a barque, two dice if it is a brigantine, or three dice if a galleon.

Add 1 to the roll if you have an excellent crew; subtract 1 if you have a poor crew.

Score 0-4	Your ship sinks	turn to **634**
Score 5-6	The mast splits	turn to **616**
Score 7-19	You weather the storm	turn to **311**

563

Choppy seas throw up fountains of white spume from the treacherous offshore rocks. Somewhere amid the hundreds of islands is the place where the Reavers keep their spoils — but it would take a master mariner to find it. Try a SCOUTING roll at a Difficulty of 15.

| Successful SCOUTING roll | turn to **653** |
| Failed SCOUTING roll | turn to **671** |

564

There are four vessels docked here at Braelak. The silk-robed captain of an Akatsurese galley is prepared to take you to Chambara for 20 Shards. A merchant whose vessel is bound for Ringhorn will take you along for 10 Shards. There is an explorer who wants 15 Shards to take you to Smogmaw. Or you can arrange passage to Aku aboard an Uttakin warship for 15 Shards.

Pay for passage to Chambara	turn to **600**
Pay for passage to Ringhorn	turn to **618**
Pay for passage to Aku	turn to **636**
Pay for passage to Smogmaw	turn to **535**
Take the road to Dweomer	turn to **175**

565

The ship slams into you and the pirates come swarming across the rail like army ants. Your crewmen stand ready to sell their lives dearly.

Roll three dice if you are a Warrior, or two dice if you belong to any other profession. Add your Rank to this roll. Then, if your crew is poor quality, subtract 2 from the total. If the crew is good, add 2. If the crew is excellent, add 3.

| Score 0-4 | Calamity; you are killed | turn to **123** |
| Score 5-9 | Crushing defeat;
lose 2-12 Stamina | turn to **435** |

Score 10-13	Forced to give in;	
	lose 1-6 Stamina	turn to **416**
Score 14-17	The pirates withdraw	turn to **32**
Score 18+	Outright victory	turn to **583**

566

The cat was the vessel's sole living crewmember. Now that you've got rid of it, you can legally help yourself to the cargo. This comprises 2 Cargo Units. Roll one die to determine the commodity.

Score 1	Minerals
Score 2	Spices
Score 3	Metals
Score 4	Textiles
Score 5	Furs
Score 6	Timber

You can add this to your own cargo if you have room on board. Then turn to **620**.

567

Your old friend Verin Crookback agrees to help you. He takes you to where your ship is lying at anchor. Your men have been pressed into service in the fields to gather produce for the Reavers' table, but with Verin's help you round up most of them and set sail under cover of darkness.

Lose the codeword *Colour* and turn to **164**.

568

Talanexor recoils in alarm. He had expected his reputation as a swift dispenser of fiery death to leave you cowed. He flicks his fingers and a globe of cold blue flames erupts from the ground at his feet.

You turn aside, dazzled, and when you look again he has gone.

Get the codeword *Cheese* and turn to **675**.

569

A narrow-hulled ship with triangular sails pulls alongside. At the rail are turbanned men from Mithdrak, a port of fabulous renown to the far west.

The merchants offer to trade cargo with you. They have 2 Cargo Units of textiles, which they are willing to exchange on a one-for-one basis for Units of furs, timber or grain.

When you have completed your business, turn to **264**.

570

You cannot make any headway. Your ship is trapped in the Sea of Reeds; each day your supplies of food and water get lower and lower.

Roll one die.

Score 1-2	You die of thirst	turn to **123**
Score 3-4	Help arrives	turn to **552**
Score 5-6	The current carries you clear	turn to **205**

571

Dweomer is the famous City of Wizards. Lining its narrow, perpetually drizzle-soaked streets are the sorcerous colleges: great gothic edifices with portals as big as those of any castle. Gargoyles stare down the rooftops, crouching below the overcast sky. It's said that some of those gargoyles are failed students.

Apply to join a college	turn to **625**
Explore the town	turn to **508**
Traverse the avenue to the docks	turn to **175**
Visit your college ☐ (if box ticked)	turn to **607**
Trade magical items	turn to **589**

572

The castaway is a merchant from Metriciens whose crew mutinied and set him ashore on the reef to die.

'May the gods harry them until the end of their days!' he says with strong feeling.

He gives you some advice on the best investments. Get the codeword *Catalyst* if you didn't have it already, then turn to **245**.

573

The Bluewood is the forest that lies south of Dweomer. The magical soil of the island has imbued the vegetation there with a strange actinic glow.

It's said that a ship whose mast is cut from a Bluewood tree will always find its way back to Braelak Isle. But the book goes on to warn of the many dangers lurking in the forest's depths, not the least of which is the Wind Spirit that can steal a man's soul.

Turn to **368**.

574

The dead man's ghost can be seen pacing the deck at night. The crew go about wide-eyed with fright.

If you cannot exorcize the ghost there will be no option but to abandon ship. For an exorcism to succeed you must make a SANCTITY roll at a Difficulty of 15.

Successful SANCTITY roll	turn to **41**
Failed SANCTITY roll	turn to **628**

575

This is no time to mince words. You utter one of the true names of the Creator – a name of such sacred force that it remorselessly divides death from life and allows no middle ground.

To see if you get it right, make a SANCTITY roll at a Difficulty of 19.

Successful SANCTITY roll	turn to **593**
Failed SANCTITY roll	turn to **484**

576 ☐

If the box above is empty, put a tick in it and turn to **229**. If the box was already ticked, turn to **599**.

577

Your prow drives into the Uttakin ship on its port side. The impact smashes its paddles, leaving the slavers unable to pursue as you sail away.

Turn to **300**.

578

You start to stammer out your reasons for coming to see him. To your dismay, the Master has risen from his chair and is staring at you very oddly. You have never seen anyone's eyes literally glow with rage before.

What will you give as your reason for disturbing him?

Ask about the Forest of Larun	turn to **632**
Ask about desert islands	turn to **596**
Ask about pirates	turn to **614**
Offer a **bottle of wine** (if you have one)	turn to **527**

579

You manage to best them in a short struggle, taking full advantage of the cramped space that prevents them from surrounding you. Soon only one of the men is still conscious. Fight him in the usual way.

Man, COMBAT 4, Defence 5, Stamina 5

Flee back to the surface	turn to **25**
Fight on and win	turn to **615**

580

If you have the blessing of Alvir and Valmir, which confers Safety from Storms, you can ignore the storm. Cross off your blessing and then turn to **32**.

Otherwise it hits with unabated fury, ripping huge waves out of the sea and flinging them across the deck. Roll one die if your ship is a barque, two dice if it is a brigantine, or three dice if it is a galleon. Add 1 to the roll if you have an excellent crew; subtract 1 if you have a poor crew.

Score 0-4	Your ship sinks	turn to **634**
Score 5-6	The mast splits	turn to **616**
Score 7+	You weather the storm	turn to **13**

581

The ship is swept far out to sea. Men and goods are washed overboard by huge waves that snap your hawsers like twine. Lose 1 Cargo Unit (if you have any cargo) and reduce your crew quality by one step – i.e. an excellent quality crew becomes good, a good quality crew becomes average, and an average quality crew becomes poor. (A poor crew can't get any worse!)

At last the storm blows itself out. You are left drifting in unknown waters.

Turn to **118**.

582

You lie down and close your eyes. What's the harm in having a short snooze until the tide turns and you can set sail? You deserve a rest...

But you and your crew are destined never to awaken. Even resurrection is no use – you are not dead, only sleeping. Cross off all codewords, ticks and notes from your Fabled Lands books and begin again with a new character.

583

You help yourself to the pirates' treasure, which amounts to 600 Shards. Record it on your Adventure Sheet. Their ship's hold contains 1 Cargo Unit of metals, which you can add to your own cargo if you have room for it.

Your mate advises taking the **pirate captain's head**. 'A grisly trophy, perhaps, but often there's a reward if you have proof you've slain such a devil.'

Your courage might also earn you another prize. Roll two dice, and if the result is greater than your current Rank then you gain a Rank. You also gain 1-6 Stamina points permanently: increase your normal (unwounded) Stamina score by the roll of one die. Remember that going up in Rank will increase your Defence by 1.

Once you have made the necessary adjustments to your Adventure Sheet, turn to **32**.

584

You pick up the **black cat**. The sailors all slope off with sullen looks.

'I suppose they think I've ruined their fun?' you remark to the bosun. 'How could you be so cruel as to even think of hurting this poor animal?'

'It wasn't for the sake of cruelty,' he protests. 'Any living thing aboard means that the ship doesn't count as abandoned, and we can't help ourselves to her cargo.'

If you are a Mage	turn to **602**
If any other profession	turn to **620**

585

Lose the codeword *Amcha* and get *Cutlass* in its place.

You know that the guildmaster will want proof that the Reaver King is dead. You slice through his neck and add **Amcha's head** to your list of possessions. Then you slip out of the citadel and hurry through the streets to the edge of town.

If you have the codeword *Crocus*, turn to **549**.

Otherwise, turn to **436**.

586

The duel is arranged for the next day, to be held in Erebus Meadow. Quite a crowd gathers in the hope of seeing some spectacular sorcery. In the event, however, Talanexor does not commence with one of his fabled fireballs. Instead, as the challenged party, he poses a conundrum. You must solve it or forfeit the duel!

'There are thirty colleges in Dweomer,' he says. 'The other day I attended a sherry party where there were six others besides myself. What was the chance that at least two of us belonged to the same college?'

What will you answer?

Twenty per cent	turn to **658**
Twenty-five per cent	turn to **694**
Fifty per cent	turn to **703**

587

The Furies seem to bear you a grudge. Your crewmen are in no hurry to get involved. While they cower below decks, you are left to fight the Furies on your own. The creatures attack you one after the other, cackling as they swing their brass-studded flails.

First Fury, COMBAT 12, Defence 19, Stamina 25

Second Fury, COMBAT 12, Defence 19, Stamina 25

Third Fury, COMBAT 12, Stamina 19, Stamina 25

There is no escape from this battle. If you defeat them all, turn to **321**.

<h1 style="text-align:center">588</h1>

Your men are pleased to see you reach the ground in one piece. You can be sure they'll sing of your heroic climb in every tavern from Krateros to Dangor. As the ship's captain who braved Starspike Island, you are sure to pass into legend. Gain 1 CHARISMA (up to a maximum of 12).

Turn to **230**.

<h1 style="text-align:center">589</h1>

After searching up and down the narrow grey streets, you find a small shop with green bottle-glass windows. A peeling gilt sign above the narrow door proudly proclaims: 'Vortense Pogue, purveyor of magical materials.'

Pogue turns out to be a thin man bound inside a tight velvet coat. He helpfully shows you his stock which, as he admits himself, is small but intriguing. (He is not interested in anything you might have to sell.)

Item	To buy
Amber wand (MAGIC +1)	500 Shards
Ebony wand (MAGIC +2)	1000 Shards
Cobalt wand (MAGIC +3)	2000 Shards
Golden katana	9000 Shards
Wizard's cape (Defence +1)	150 Shards
Parrot fungus	250 Shards
Black cat	20 Shards
Parchment	1 Shard
Candle	2 Shards

Steal an item	turn to **643**
Finish your business and go	turn to **571**

<h1 style="text-align:center">590</h1>

The men applaud your nobility in staying with them no matter what fate has in store. Gain 1 point of CHARISMA, up to the maximum limit of 12. Then roll one die.

Score 1-2	The others all die of thirst	turn to **700**
Score 3-4	Fever breaks out	turn to **611**
Score 5-6	The wind picks up	turn to **155**

591

The key of stars opens the sealed gates of the Tower of Despair, which the book you are reading locates in the Forest of the Forsaken — not, as popular myth would have it, on the banks of the Rese River.

The key appears to have passed through many hands across the centuries, but is now believed to be in the possession of the Trau King of the Whistling Heath.

Turn to **368**.

592

The Kraken returns to the depths, inexorably dragging your vessel down with it. Cross the ship and crew off your Ship's Manifest. They are lost; you will be lucky if you can save yourself.

Roll two dice. If the score is greater than your Rank, you are drowned — turn to **123**. If the score is less than or equal to your Rank, you are swept miraculously towards a beach of soft white sand. Lose 2-12 Stamina points and (if you can survive that) turn to **111** in *The Lone and Level Sands*.

593

Upon hearing the name of the first of the gods, the skeletons burst asunder and fall clattering to the deck. Your men flatly refuse to cross to the other vessel, which is now slowly slipping below the waves in any case, but among the heap of bones you find a **sword (COMBAT +6)** and a suit of **splint armour (Defence +4)**.

After noting your new possessions, turn to **321**.

594

You give a stirring speech that turns them around completely. Soon they are vowing to follow your orders to the ends of the earth.

`Aye, and beyond!' declares the bosun. `As far as hell's harbour gates, if you ask us, skipper!'

Roll two dice, and if you get more than your CHARISMA score then increase it by 1. Acquire the codeword *Curdle* and turn to **282**.

595

Your prow drives into the side of the Uttakin ship, which is unable to turn fast enough to avoid the collision. Water pours in through the broken timbers. With the weight of its metal flanks, the vessel is pulled down into the depths.

A few survivors come swimming across calling for mercy. Your crew club the Uttakin unconscious and loot their belongings. There are also a few slaves who managed to slip out of their bonds as the ship went down. They are wealthy merchants from Metriciens who reward you handsomely for bringing about their rescue. All in all, you gain 450 Shards from the encounter. Add this to the sum on your Adventure Sheet, then turn to **300**.

596

'Why not see for yourself? There is no substitute for practical experience!' cries the Master, hurling a spell at you. There is a moment of nauseating weightlessness, your surroundings drop away, and then you are floundering about in the sea close to a palm-fringed beach. Turn to **505**.

597

One of the men gets behind you and gives you a 'Ringhorn love tap' on the back of the head with his cudgel. You sigh and swoon.

You wake up in the bilges of a ship. Your possessions and money are gone. Also cross off your ship if you had one; you will not see your faithful crew again.

You have been enslaved by smugglers from Uttaku.

Leap overboard	turn to **158**
Stay on the ship	*The Court of Hidden Faces* **321**

598

The sky is the colour of burning sulphur. From behind the clouds comes the growl of thunder. The sailors mutter in fear.

'It is the wrath of Elnir,' says the mate. 'He summons us to our doom!'

If you have the blessing of Alvir and Valmir, which confers Safety from Storms, you can ignore the storm. Cross off your blessing and turn to **50**.

Otherwise the storm hits with titanic fury, flinging mighty waves across the deck. Roll one die if your ship is a barque, two dice if it is a brigantine, or three dice if a galleon. Add 1 to the roll if you have an excellent crew; subtract 1 if you have a poor crew.

Score 0-4	Your ship sinks	turn to **634**
Score 5-6	The mast splits	turn to **670**
Score 7-19	You weather the storm	turn to **9**

599

Sneering at your feeble excuses, the men set you ashore on a deserted island.

'How do you expect me to survive?' you ask them.

'What business is it of ours if you live or die?' is their callous reply.

Turn to **177**.

600

The ship steers out of harbour and sets her prow to the east. Cross off the 20 Shards if you haven't already, then roll one die.

Score 1	Shipwreck; you alone reach land. Turn to **505**
Score 2-6	You reach Chambara safely. Turn to paragraph **79** in *Lords of the Rising Sun*

601

An icy downpour forces you to shelter in a lonely barn where you are reduced to eating some of the fodder left for the animals. By daybreak you have a fever, and are in no condition to put up a fight when you are discovered by the owner of the barn.

'The Reavers will give me a reward for capturing you,' he says.

Turn to **472**.

602

You may not be able to take the ghost ship's cargo, but you get another kind of reward for saving the cat's life.

Roll two dice. If the total exceeds your MAGIC score, you gain 1 point of MAGIC. Then turn to **32**.

603

You have the advantage of surprise. The pirates stand slack-jawed as they see you bounding down the hill, and your men take advantage of the diversion to arm themselves with planks, chains, belaying pins – whatever comes to hand. But the pirates have swords and armour.

Make a COMBAT roll at Difficulty 16. (You can add 2 to the dice roll if you have an excellent crew.)

Successful COMBAT roll	turn to **457**
Failed COMBAT roll	turn to **123**

604

He tosses a globe of magical fire at your back. Lose 3-18 Stamina points. It would have been worse if not for the mist, which helped stifle the flames.

If still alive, you manage to escape from Talanexor down a narrow alley, but now you have lost sight of Lauria.

Turn to **571**.

605

The Furies raise their brass-studded whips and give you a lashing just to instil moral rectitude. Then, as the sun emerges again, they fly off cackling with laughter. Where their feet touched the deck there are bloody prints that no amount of scrubbing will clean away.

Lose 2-12 Stamina points for the whipping and, if you survive, turn to **321**.

606

Anyone who has climbed a mountain knows that it is easier to go up than to come down. Your heart is in your mouth as you make the perilous descent.

Make a SCOUTING roll at a Difficulty of 15 to climb down safely.

You can add 1 to the dice roll if you have a **rope**; add 2 if you have **climbing gear**.

Successful SCOUTING roll	turn to **588**
Failed SCOUTING roll	turn to **123**

607

If you like, your college will hold possessions and money here for safe-keeping. Record in the box anything that you wish to leave here. Each time you return, roll two dice.

Score 2-10	Your possessions and money are safe
Score 11-12	College fees mean that 10% of money left here has been deducted

ITEMS AT COLLEGE

You can also reside in college for as long as you wish, making use of the infirmary if need be. (If injured, restore your Stamina to its normal unwounded score.)

Call on the Master	turn to **207**
Visit the kitchens	turn to **187**
Study	turn to **696**
Research	turn to **368**
Leave	turn to **571**

608

'Were you set ashore by your fellow crewmen?' you ask the poor wretch, for this is a common punishment at sea.

'No,' he says. 'We had the misfortune to encounter a shoal of mermaids. Hearing their sad sweet song, all the others flung themselves into the sea and were drowned. Later the ship hit that reef and sank, and there I waited till you found me.'

'Why didn't the mermaids' song affect you?'

He gives a wry smile. 'I'm tone deaf.'

Get the codeword *Cynosure* and turn to **245**.

609

Estragon is the court wizard of Baroness Ravayne of Golnir. He was formerly the Warden of Choronzon College here in Dweomer, but left under something of a cloud.

'That would have been his experiment in storm magic,' elucidates the librarian. 'I remember it rained for thirteen months and a day.'

'Heavy rain, presumably?'

He nods. 'The High Street was accessible only by punt, and the Warden of Cromlech College drowned after falling asleep in his wine cellar.'

'And what does Estragon do these days?' you ask.

'Continues his experiments, I hear. Adventurers who help him out with various quests are richly rewarded.'

Turn to **368**.

610

Along with some of your officers, you manage to lower the cutter and row off. The Kraken sinks down into the depths carrying the shattered remnants of your ship with it.

It is with bitter heart that you abandon the men crying for help in the water, but there is not enough room in the cutter for all of them. (Remember to cross off the details on your Ship's Manifest.)

After several days you drift in to the shelter of a quiet bay. Your officers rest in the shade of a row of coconut palms, but to your dismay it is impossible to wake them later. Only then do you realize you must have landed on the fateful Sleeping Isle.

The cutter is too much for you to handle alone. You break it up for firewood and to build yourself a shelter. You may be on this island for some time.

Turn to **177**.

611

One of the men falls ill. His skin turns yellow and he begins to vomit, and death follows quickly. The plague spreads, the narrow confines of the ship allowing no escape for any of you. You watch the crew die in front of your eyes.

Unless you have a blessing of Immunity to Disease/Poison you soon succumb yourself: turn to **123**. If you have such a blessing, cross it off and turn to **700**.

612

Over the past few days you have had cause to reduce rations and enforce some stern discipline. Now the men are getting unruly. You must address them and hope to sway them with the force of your personality.

Make a CHARISMA roll at a Difficulty of 13.

Successful CHARISMA roll	turn to **594**
Failed CHARISMA roll	turn to **576**

613

You are stripped of your money and possessions. Cross them off your Adventure Sheet. Also cross off your ship — the Uttakin scupper it. Along with the surviving members of your crew, you are locked in shackles.

The Uttakin captain looks down on you with an inscrutable stare.

'Forget your former life,' he advises you. 'Now and forevermore you are a slave.'

Turn to **321** in *The Court of Hidden Faces*.

614

'A good question!' The Master titters with rather unbalanced laughter. 'Go and take a look. You might gain some useful material for a thesis.'

He throws a spell and a bolt of blackness surrounds you. Slowly it fades, revealing that you are wallowing in the surf close to a barren stretch of shoreline. Turn to **313**.

615

Checking the crates, you discover bottles of Harkunan brandy wine.

Obviously the men were smugglers, and the note about spectral hauntings was just a ploy to scare the miners away from where they kept their contraband.

You can take a **bottle of wine**, a **deck of marked cards**, four **cudgels** and the 117 Shards the smugglers had on them. Then you return to the surface; turn to **25**.

616

The ship is swept far out to sea. Men and goods are washed overboard by huge waves that snap your hawsers like twine. Lose 1 Cargo Unit (if you have any cargo) and reduce your crew quality by one step – i.e. an excellent crew becomes good, a good crew becomes average, and an average crew becomes poor.

At last the storm blows itself out. You are left drifting in unknown waters. Turn to **50**.

617

He is Alkeides, a warrior from the distant city-state of Krateros, cursed by the gods to die by his brother's hand.

'Naturally, when my ship sank I was unable to drown. I have been trying to get to my homeland so that I might entreat the gods to lift the curse, or else put an honourable end to my days. But each storm raises the sea and flings me to and fro.'

You help out by dropping him at the next port, where he may be able to find a ship to carry him home.

Get the codeword *Cithara* and turn to **116**.

618

Remember to pay the 10 Shards that is the cost of passage to Ringhorn. The ship is soon under way. Roll a die.

Score 1	Storms force you south to Brazen; turn to **99**
Score 2-6	You reach Ringhorn without difficulty; turn to **2** in *Cities of Gold and Glory*

619

It is a high-prowed merchant ship from Akatsurai, distinguishable by its triangular sails and the golden sun symbol displayed on the aft deck.

The ship comes alongside and the captain invites you aboard. He chats to you for a while about trade between his country and Golnir.

If you are a Warrior, turn to **519**. Otherwise you sail on; turn to **228**.

620

You sail away from the deserted ship. 'I wonder what happened to her crew?' you wonder.

The mate gives a shudder. `Eerie things abound in these waters, captain,' he replies.

Turn to **32**.

621

After a year of piracy you have risen to the rank of captain. You put it to your men that with the spoils you've collected it would be better to turn to honest work. `Why live like robbers until our luck runs out? We can be princes in Metriciens!'

They agree and the booty is divided up. Your share comes to 8500 Shards and a **sword (COMBAT +4)**. Decide where you want to make your home.

In Wishport	*Cities of Gold and Glory* **217**
In Dweomer	turn to **571**
In Smogmaw	turn to **44**
In Yellowport	*The War-Torn Kingdom* **10**

622

You bump into somebody in the mist – a tall gentleman in a velvet cape. `Excuse me.' You go to move past him; you don't want Lauria to get away.

He plants a thin hand on your chest. `A moment of your time. I think we are old acquaintances?'

You shake your head. `I don't believe so.'

`No? In that case,' he asks with a twitch of his thin lips, `why did you make yourself at home in my house?'

You give him a closer look. `Who?'

`I am Talanexor the Fireweaver, you scoundrel. And your name, I believe, is Lauria.'

You start to protest. `I'm not Lauria! She's just gone that way. If we hurry we can catch her.'

He gives a hollow laugh. `You must think me a fool. Prepare to take your punishment.'

Fight him	turn to **568**
Challenge him to a duel	turn to **586**
Run off	turn to **604**

623

After a drunken argument in the mess, one of the sailors is found with his brains battered out. There seems no doubt about the man responsible – a bloody rag is found hidden under his bunk and he is known for his explosive temper.

Order him thrown overboard	turn to **536**
Let the incident pass	turn to **554**

624

The men lie around the deck waiting to die. Your tongue is sticking to the roof of your mouth now, and your vision is blurred with hunger.

'Sweet heaven, skipper,' croaks the bosun, 'must we die too?'

Take the officers and escape in the rowboat	turn to **520**
Stay with your ship to the bitter end	turn to **590**

625

There are many colleges, each distinguished in its own field. Fortuity College has a high reputation in the study of charms and benedictions. Carminry College is for the study of magic as a means of curing illness. Fulgur College specializes in the conjuring of storms. And so on…

Whichever college you decide to apply for, the procedure is the same. First you are subjected to an examination which decides how holy you are. You have to try to drive off a vexatious sprite using only a display of self-righteous indignation, wax pompously on the topic of other people's ethics, curdle milk with a beatific smile, speculate uselessly for hours on what the gods really intended when they made Man, and so forth.

Make a SANCTITY roll at a Difficulty of 14.

Successful SANCTITY roll	turn to **661**
Failed SANCTITY roll	turn to **679**

626

There is a ghostly howl that makes your hair stand on end. Unable to remain another moment in this uncanny place, you hurry back downstairs into the open air. Turn to **407**.

627

You find an extract in the *Wondrous Annals of Nic O'Carmolop, Master Mariner*:

'In the great forests of that southern land known as Ankon-Konu abide creatures whose like is not found elsewhere at any part of the world. In the higher branches there are fungi that can float on the warm breezes and ensnare monkeys and birds. With my own eyes I beheld a man slain by the crimson moss which can grow in great swathes overnight, suffocating the unwary. In leafy groves as dark as caverns I met with men whose eyes were like great jewels atop their heads. There are insects as hard and bright as glass, large as a man's fist, and monkeys with the morals of a Metriciens street-thug. But strangest of all are the creatures that give Ankon-Konu the name by which mariners commonly know it. These creatures are the plumed flying fish of the jungle, and the name by which the continent is thus called is the Feathered Lands.'

'Not all authorities agree,' says the librarian, looking over your shoulder. 'I have heard other, quite different, accounts of that land.' Turn to **368**.

628

It is with heavy heart that you scupper the ship, putting to sea in the rowboats. After several weeks at sea you are reduced to eating worm-ridden biscuits and drinking rainwater. At last Smogmaw comes in sight. You put in at the quayside and stagger ashore, too weary to notice that the current is carrying your rowboats back out to sea.

Cross your ship and cargo off the Ship's Manifest. You will have to lay off the crew as well because there are no vessels for immediate purchase here in Smogmaw. Turn to **44**.

629

Some of the items stored on deck were not properly lashed down, and got swept overboard during the night. Lose one Cargo Unit if you are carrying any cargo — if you have more than one Unit, you can choose which is lost. If you had no cargo, lose 1-6 of your possessions instead.

Now turn to **190**.

630

At sunset the water develops a deep shadowy tinge. It is this that gives the Violet Ocean its name. On the horizon, clouds lie in long lines against the blood-drenched sky like the ranks of a distant army. Roll two dice.

Score 2-4	Pirates	turn to **666**
Score 5-6	Storm	turn to **355**
Score 7-12	An uneventful voyage	turn to **648**

631

You step up to the great bronze door. Perched on a nearby rock, rigid as a sculpture, you notice a lizard glaring with wide, sightless eyes. Make a MAGIC roll at a Difficulty of 10.

Successful MAGIC roll	turn to **667**
Failed MAGIC roll	turn to **121**

632

'I knew it!' he shrieks. 'The librarian sent you, didn't he? Well, just you tell him that I'll keep it as long as I want. I'm the Master! Me!'

He flicks a spell of summary dispatch. The room disappears, there is a whirling kaleidoscope around you, then you find yourself plummeting out of a clear sky to land with a thud at the base of a tall oak.

Turn to **596** in *The War-Torn Kingdom*.

633

You retrace your steps until you are standing beside the shaft that the mine supervisor had boarded up. The tunnel you are in stretches back to the surface.

Go deeper into the mine	turn to **651**
Head for the surface	turn to **394**

<h1 style="text-align:center">634</h1>

Helpless in the grip of the storm, the vessel cracks apart. The seawater rushes into the broken shell of the hull, dragging you down. The screams of your crewmen are drowned out by the howl of the storm. Cross the ship and crew off your Ship's Manifest. You can think of nothing now but saving yourself.

Roll two dice. If the score is greater than your Rank, you are drowned – turn to **123**. If the score is less than or equal to your Rank, you are swept miraculously towards a rocky shore. Lose 2-12 Stamina points and (if you can survive that) turn to **559** in *Cities of Gold and Glory*.

<h1 style="text-align:center">635</h1>

It is a priest of Elnir, who is gaining religious merit by walking between the many shrines and temples of his deity. 'Faith keeps my feet dry,' he says. 'And devotion keeps my head pointed to the sky.'

He delivers a stirring sermon that inspires your crew. If the crew were of poor quality, upgrade them to average.

Also, if you are an initiate of Elnir, the priest gives you a **healing salve (restores 1-6 Stamina)** which you can list among your possessions. It can be used *once* when you are injured to give back one die roll of Stamina points. After use, cross it off. The priest bids you good day and goes strolling off across the sea. Turn to **116**.

<h1 style="text-align:center">636</h1>

The ship manoeuvres out on to open ocean and is soon heading north under a full press of sail. Pay the 15 Shards for your berth if you haven't already, then roll one die.

Score 1	Captured by slavers; turn to **321** in *The Court of Hidden Faces*
Score 2	The ship goes down in a storm, but you cling to a raft; turn to **180**
Score 3-6	You reach Aku without incident; turn to **444** in *The Court of Hidden Faces*

<h1 style="text-align:center">637</h1>

It isn't much of a boat – just bundles of twigs and bracken lashed together to make a kind of crude pontoon. With fair weather and the kindness of the gods you might just stay afloat long enough to reach civilization.

Roll one die; you can add 1 to the roll if you are a Wayfarer.

Score 1-2	The boat sinks	turn to **123**
Score 3-4	Picked up by pirates	turn to **472**
Score 5	Swept ashore on an island	turn to **505**
Score 6-7	Reach a port	turn to **673**

638

You are chained to the wall of the Reaver King's throne room and flogged whenever he is in a bad temper – which is often. Days turn into weeks and gradually your health declines. Lose 3-18 Stamina points. If you survive, there eventually comes a time when you are too weak and battered to give the Reavers any sport. They sell you to slavers from Yarimura, who strip you of any possessions and money you may have managed to hold on to.

Lose the codewords *Crocus* or *Colour* if you have them, then turn to **357** in *The Plains of Howling Darkness*.

639

You push your luck too far. You have many enemies – among them a wealthy silk merchant who lost several of his shipments during your last outing as a pirate. He sets a price on your head that brings bounty hunters from all across the known world, and within a month you have been taken at sea. Your execution comes soon after. Turn to **123**.

640

The scholars demand half of any cash you're carrying. (If you have no cash they will take the first two possessions listed on your Adventure Sheet.) They euphemistically describe this as moonlight tax, even though mist or drizzle mean it is rarely possible to see the moon in Dweomer. Now turn to **571**.

641

The curse is not long in taking effect. 'Yuck!' says the first mate, spitting out the water he had taken from the barrel on deck. 'It's gone scummy!'

Turn to **124**.

642

You climb so high that the atmosphere itself drops away. You are surrounded by thousands of stars shining like diamonds in a midnight blue firmament.

At the summit of the mountain is a gateway of wrought iron fastened with a padlock. You will need a **fretwork key** or a THIEVERY roll at Difficulty 20 to unlock it.

Unlock the gate	turn to **497**
Can't unlock it	turn to **606**

643

Not wise. Do you think no one ever tried that before? The panel of a large grandfather clock snaps open, a long scaly arm shoots out and grabs your neck, and you are pulled through into a dank indistinct place where you are rapidly stripped of your possessions (cross them off your Adventure Sheet). That done, the arm flings you down on a cold stone floor before vanishing.

Turn to **415**.

644

The casket breaks to fragments under your enchanted touch. You take the **celestium wand (MAGIC +5)** and then hurry excitedly back outside, eager to test the power of your new acquisition.

Add the **celestium wand (MAGIC +5)** to your list of possessions, then turn to **407**.

645

If half of what you read about Akatsurai is true, it must be one of the strangest countries of the world.

The knights of Akatsurai (who are known as samurai) are utterly without fear, striving gladly for death if only they can win honour with their last breath. In fact, honour is so highly prized that a samurai threatened with disgrace usually opts to take his own life by slitting open his belly with a dagger.

The samurai are the rulers of Akatsurai, and any samurai can slay any peasant with no better reason than to test the edge of his sword! The chief of all the samurai is called the Shogun, whose court is in Chambara.

There is also an Emperor, but according to most accounts he wields little true power.

Also worth noting is a small and secretive sect of wizardly assassins which is active in the remote rural areas. They are known as ninja, a word which literally means Masters of Invisibility.

Turn to **368**.

646

The island turns out to be the back of a sea-going behemoth that has basked in the sun for so long that vegetation has started to grow on it. Woken by the tread of your boots, the creature issues forth an angry waterspout and dives beneath the waves.

Several of your men are lost in the mad scramble back aboard the ship. Reduce your ship's Crew Quality to poor and turn to **283**.

647

Hundred-headed hydras arise from the sea on all sides. Hissing venomously, they lash out to seize men from the decks. Roll two dice; add 2 if your Crew Quality is excellent, add 1 if it is good, and subtract 2 if it is poor.

Score 0-3	Everyone is killed; turn to **123**
Score 4-6	You alone survive; turn to **700**
Score 7-9	Many losses; reduce Crew Quality to poor and turn to **118**
Score 10+	The hydras are driven off; turn to **448**

648

You are far out at sea with no land in sight.

'The Feathered Lands lie south of here,' the helmsman mutters, 'but will we ever see them? Not this side of the grave, I'll wager!' You distract him from such gloomy thoughts by ordering a new course.

Steer north towards Golnir	turn to **504**
Steer south to Ankon-Konu	turn to **189**
Steer east	turn to **42**
Steer west	turn to **244**

649

On the clifftop above the door you discover a sinkhole with a faint glow of lamplight shining up from below. Lowering yourself down, you soon reach a cavern where two tall women with serpentine tresses are pacing to and fro like hungry cats.

`Sister, there is a fresh mortal in our land,' says one.

The other nods, causing the snakes of her head to hiss softly. `Yes, I feel it too. Tomorrow we shall hunt.'

Leave while you can	turn to **342**
Creep in when they're asleep	turn to **432**

650

Dangor is a city east of the Gashmuru Gulf. It stands atop cliffs hundreds of metres high, and you are particularly intrigued by the account of one Horbel Humbing, Master Mariner, of the HMS *Sokar*: `We arrived at the base of the cliffs and there laid at anchor three days, while a mountaineer carried our documents to the port authorities above. These documents being found to be in order, grapples were lowered and secured and the whole vessel was winched up to the docks a thousand feet above.'

Turn to **368**.

651 ☐

If the box above is empty, put a tick in it and turn to **686**. If it was already ticked, turn to **358**.

652

Gaspar will invest money for you in various enterprises. The investment must be in multiples of 100 Shards. Write the sum you are investing in the box here (or withdraw a sum invested previously) and then turn to **687.**

MONEY INVESTED

653

You manage to avoid smashing your ship open on the reefs, but you are no closer to locating the secret bay where the Reavers store their booty. You decide to put in at a fishing village and see if you can get anything out of the locals.

To gain their confidence you will need to either succeed in a CHARISMA roll at Difficulty 12 or show them a **silver medallion**.

Gain their confidence	turn to **688**
Failed attempt at CHARISMA	turn to **701**

654

A pirate galley comes bucking across the waves, gaining steadily in the mild breeze.

'If the wind doesn't pick up, we're done for!' shouts the helmsman.

Make a run for it	turn to **672**
Parley	turn to **689**
Fight it out	turn to **361**

655

At the back of a wide bay you find a town which rises with steep streets to a grim citadel. The blood-coloured flag of the Reavers flies from the battlements. In the harbour, a dozen pirate ships ride at anchor.

Walk openly into the town	turn to **114**
Sneak in at night	turn to **362**
Make a getaway	turn to **380**

656

The Reavers hold a banquet in the great hall of their stronghold. The finest wines are served – wines of southern Sokara that were intended for the cellars of the merchant princes of Metriciens. The meat is flavoured with the exotic spices of distant lands, and there are sweetmeats from Chrysoprais and nuts from Ankon-Konu. These Reavers dine like kings!

If you have the codeword *Amcha*, turn to **674**. If not, turn to **691**.

657

Passing the latticed windows of a tavern, you happen to glance inside

where you see a tall young woman having dinner with an older man
who has a scholarly look about him. You walk on a few steps and then
stop as if struck by a thunderbolt. The woman is Lauria, the thief who
twice played you for a fool. You swore you'd get even with her one day!

Go inside and confront her	turn to **692**
Wait for her to leave	turn to **702**
Swallow your pride and forget it	turn to **571**

658

It is rather disheartening the way all the onlookers sigh and shake their
heads the moment you give your answer.

'Talanexor always gets them with that one!' you overhear an old
professor saying.

Having been judged loser in the dispute you have brought shame on
your college if you belong to one, and are forthwith expelled. Turn to
571 – and remember to erase the tick in the college box if there is one
there.

659 ☐

If the box above is empty, put a tick in it and turn to **51**. If it was already
ticked, turn to **623**.

660

You are in trouble. Roll one die.

Score 1-2	You slip and fall	turn to **123**
Score 3-4	You are forced to give up	turn to **230**
Score 5-6	You make a final effort	turn to **695**

661

The examiners are thirteen astoundingly old men in dusty black robes. They sit at a long table studying the results of your first exam. Minutes tick by, then you hear a low snoring sound.

The senior mage raps his knuckles on the table, gathers some papers, and peers down at you.

'We can't admit you to the college,' he wheezes. 'You're just too insufferably sanctimonious. You need to have an open mind to study wizardry, you know.'

You start to leave, but then another of the wizards says: 'Wait. We can't have you going straight off to bother another college.'

He casts a spell of transportation and you are flung magically across a thousand leagues in the blink of an eye, landing in a dungheap outside the town of Smogmaw. Turn to **44**.

662

A ghost has gathered substance from the magical residue in the air here. It pounces to attack you with claws as sharp as the north wind during a thaw.

Ghost, COMBAT 8, Defence 17, Stamina 7

If you flee it will flay the flesh off your back, inflicting 1-6 Stamina points.

Flee from the tower	turn to **407**
Fight on and win	turn to **626**

663

The trau are a subterranean race, the remnants of the gods' first abortive attempts to create man. They have a reputation for surliness, disliking to mix with mankind because they are jealous of man's more perfect visage and well-fashioned form. However, the trau are skilled at metal-working and will sometimes sell trinkets of exquisite workmanship for nothing more than a sip of faery mead. Turn to **368**.

664

Fresh roasted sea-fowl makes a welcome supplement to your customary diet of gruel, ship's biscuit and weevils. Recover 1-6 Stamina points if injured (the score of one die) and then turn to **283**.

665

A thick white fog billows across the sea during the night. The first mate rouses you from sleep to show you an eerie scene that is unfolding by moonlight. The rays of the moon, illuminating the drifting tendrils of fog, create the appearance of a vast lake from which warriors are slowly arising as if after a deep sleep.

'It puts me in mind of a legend I heard,' breathes the mate in a low voice. 'It's said the High King and his paladins lie beneath the Rimewater, awaiting the one whose destiny it is to awaken them.'

As he speaks a gust of wind stirs the fog, breaking up the fragile illusion. Turn to **264**.

666

A pirate galley bears down on you with the swift ferocity of a panther scenting a kill.

Make a run for it	turn to **684**
Parley	turn to **373**
Fight it out	turn to **392**

667

Not having been born yesterday, you have the forethought to tear a strip of cloth off your tunic and wind it across your eyes before knocking. As the echoes of your knock die away, there is a creak of vast time-worn hinges and a gust of stale air that tells you the doors have opened in front of you.

'Another one,' says a cold hissing voice, not much like a woman's.

'When will they learn not to beard the Gorgons in their lair?' crows her sister.

Charge to attack them	turn to **685**
Stand motionless	turn to **356**

668

The Shadar were the race that ruled Harkuna in ancient times. The time of their reign is thought of as a golden age, where peace and harmony encouraged a flowering of arts and sciences. They were overthrown by the coming of the Uttakin, but some culture still survives in the form of hoary tradition.

Turn to **368**.

669

The spectres abandon their macabre frolics to fall upon you with terrible whispering cries. Fingers of icy mist seep into your flesh. In a trice your soul has been severed from your body.

Turn to **123**.

670

The ship is swept far out to sea. Men and goods are washed overboard by huge waves that snap your hawsers like twine. Lose 1 Cargo Unit (if you have any cargo) and reduce your crew quality by one step – i.e. an excellent crew becomes good, a good crew becomes average, and an average crew becomes poor. (A poor crew can't get any worse!)

At last the storm blows itself out. You are left drifting in unknown waters.

Turn to **648**.

671

'Merciful gods!' you cry in exasperation as you shuffle your sea charts. 'How many of these cursed islands are there?'

'They are numberless, cap'n,' says the first mate gravely. 'That is why the navies of Sokara and Golnir have had no success in dealing with these pirates. It is impossible to find their base of operations.'

Roll two dice.

Score 2	You find it by luck	turn to **545**
Score 3-6	The Reavers find you	turn to **354**
Score 7-8	You hit a reef	turn to **249**
Score 9-12	You reach open ocean	turn to **164**

672

Roll two dice and add your Rank. Add 1 to the total if you have an average crew, add 2 if you have a good crew, or add 3 if you have an excellent crew.

Score 1-6	The pirates overtake you	turn to **361**
Score 7+	You outrun them	turn to **311**

673

The boat is so waterlogged that you have to abandon it and swim to the quayside. An old man carrying a lobster pot helps you up and you ask him where you are.

He points along an avenue lined with strange black statues. At the far end is a city of many high turrets, the stone gleaming like gold under an indigo sky.

'This is Braelak Isle. Yon city is Dweomer.'

Turn to **100**.

674

The Guildmaster in Marlock City promised a reward if you brought him the head of Amcha One-Eye.

Go through with the plan to kill Amcha	turn to **420**
Let him live for now	turn to **691**

675

You are just passing the steps of Sinistrum College when you are set upon by three scholars. They have turned to robbery as a way of supplementing their meagre grants but, being of good families, your assailants are sporting enough to fight you one at a time.

First Scholar, COMBAT 3, Defence 4, Stamina 3

Second Scholar, COMBAT 4, Defence 5, Stamina 4

Third Scholar, COMBAT 3, Defence 4, Stamina 4

Surrender	turn to **640**
Fight on and win	turn to **571**

676

'Ah, this is a stroke of luck,' calls the captain of the royalist vessel. 'We were sent to find you. The High King charges you to bring him a fragment of **selenium ore**.'

You bow politely. 'Please assure our lord that I go at once to do his bidding.'

The other ship sails off. Turn to **475**.

677

The crew is on the verge of mutiny. You must assert your authority if you hope to avoid a disaster. Make a CHARISMA roll at a Difficulty of 15.

Successful CHARISMA roll	turn to **188**
Failed CHARISMA roll	turn to **599**

678

Wisps of cloud swirl around you. When you gaze down, the tiny figures of your men are like midges beside the great basin of the sea. The altitude is making you dizzy.

If you have the codeword *Calcium*, turn to **642**. If not, the increasingly thin air forces you to turn back – turn to **606**.

679

The Master of the College has you in for a sherry. Waving you to a deep leather armchair that makes a serious bid at engorging you, he scans your exam papers and says: 'You seem unsure about anything at all. Most of the metaphysical questions you've just answered with a Don't Know. The sprite liked you so much that it's taken up residence in your coat pocket – and your smile, instead of curdling the milk, almost froze it.'

You look at him uncertainly. 'Does that mean—?'

He grins and seizes your hand. 'You'll be a model student! Welcome to the college.'

Turn to **571** and put a tick in the box by the college option there.

680   ☐

You reach the chamber at the top of the tower.

If the box above was already ticked, immediately turn to **662**.

If the box is empty there is a wand sealed here inside a crystalline casket. You can attempt to open it by making a MAGIC roll at Difficulty 16.

If you succeed, put a tick in the box and then turn to **644**. If you fail, leave the box empty and turn to **626**. Or you can just leave the tower, turn to **407**.

681

The Uttakin originally came across the seas from the south, a warrior race that subjugated the land of Old Harkuna and put the High King to the sword for daring to oppose them. But that was almost three centuries ago. Factional infighting wasted the strength of the Uttakin. Civilization sapped the conquering spirit of the once-proud people, and their ancient rituals became decadent and devoid of meaning. Now they rule only the land of Uttaku, their energies devoted solely to elaborate courtly intrigues and internecine plotting. The courtiers are said to wear masks that symbolically display the wearer's prestige and power while concealing his true feelings. The king is that one man in every generation who is actually born without a face…

You close your books with a shudder. Turn to **368**.

682

The entire island is carpeted in a mossy grey-green sward. Freshwater has collected in hollows in the ground and there are tame birds that you can easily catch to eat.

Roll one die.

Score 1	turn to **646**
Score 2-6	turn to **664**

683

You wake up to find that every man on board lies dead and cold, with the sole exception of yourself. You are at a loss to explain how this ghastly tragedy could have come about – or why you should have been spared. Turn to **700**.

684

Roll two dice and add your Rank. Add 1 to the total if you have an average crew, 2 if you have a good crew, or 3 if you have an excellent crew.

Score 1-6	The pirates overtake you	turn to **392**
Score 7+	You outrun them	turn to **648**

685

This promises to be a desperate struggle, but at least you have a fighting chance – if you could clearly see the Gorgons' eyes, on the other hand, it would all be over in an instant. Fight them one after the other.

First Gorgon, COMBAT 4, Defence 5, Stamina 8

Second Gorgon, COMBAT 5, Defence 6, Stamina 11

There is nowhere to flee. If you win, turn to **393**.

686

'A copper thief, eh?' snarls a trau who has been employed to work the seam here. He launches himself at you, a burly blot against the darkness, hands like shovels, eyes glossy black like a huge moth's.

Trau Miner, COMBAT 8, Defence 10, Stamina 10

If you win, turn to **376**.

687

Mist swirls down the narrow alleys and loiters in darkened doorways. The streetlamps give off a haloed gleam because of it.

If you have the codeword *Anger*, turn to **657**. Otherwise turn to **675**.

688

The fishermen take you to the village alehouse, where drink and good company soon loosen their wary tongues.

'We are a privileged community,' boasts one old man, 'for we are situated close to the Reavers citadel and are often called on to provide food and drink for their table.'

Before long you have a good idea how to find the Reavers' secret bay. Bidding the villagers goodnight, you return to your ship.

Get the codeword *Chance* and turn to **545**.

689

The ship pulls alongside. The pirates cast out grappling hooks and within moments are swarming aboard. You offer them your goods in exchange for your freedom.

Make a CHARISMA roll at a Difficulty of 15.

Successful CHARISMA roll	turn to **416**
Failed CHARISMA roll	turn to **435**

690

If you have the codeword *Amcha*, turn to **420**. If not, turn to **287**.

691

The feast goes on late into the night, and dawn finds most of the pirates slumped across the tables. A few hardy souls are still stuffing titbits into their mouths, swilling them down with Uttakin brandy. 'So, is it your intention to take up the piratical life yourself?' asks one man.

If you have the codeword *Crocus*, turn to **549**. If not but you have the codeword *Colour*, turn to **458**. Otherwise turn to **476**.

692 ☐

If the box above is empty, put a tick in it and turn to **364**. If the box was already ticked, turn to **382**.

693

During an eclipse, when the sun is hidden and day becomes night, hideous straggle-haired crones with leathery wings suddenly drop out of the sky uttering shrill cries.

If you have the codeword *Judas*, turn to **587**. If not, turn to **605**.

694

Talanexor laughs triumphantly. The spectators grumble disappointedly and start to wander off.

'Is that it?' you ask anyone who'll listen.

'Talanexor always does that,' replies an aged college servant. 'He's too stingy to buy the expensive ingredients he needs for fire magic, you see.'

As loser of the dispute you are judged guilty of burgling Talanexor's home and must pay him all your cash. Then turn to **571**.

695

The lower slopes are slippery with moss, but after a while you find the going easier. The rock is hard, with deep gouges that provide you with secure handholds. Make a SCOUTING roll at Difficulty 13. Add 1 to the dice roll if you possess a **rope**, or add 2 if you have **climbing gear**.

Successful SCOUTING roll	turn to **678**
Failed SCOUTING roll	turn to **660**

696

'It's good to see you remember to turn up at lectures once in a while,' remarks the senior mage drily as you sidle in at the back of the hall.

You must pay 200 Shards in tutorial fees, then roll two dice. If you get higher than your current MAGIC score, increase it by 1. However, if you roll a 2 then you have got things so badly wrong that you lose 1 point of MAGIC. That done, turn to **607**.

697

The bark of the trees has a deep indigo colour, and the leaves sparkle with azure light. Things slither amid the shadows, elusive as memories of old dreams.

Search for a way out	turn to **388**
Press on deeper into the wood	turn to **408**

698

Here is the entry you find in an old book that is yellow with age.

'Once the pinnacle of civilization in the northlands, Old Harkuna is now but a wrecked shell of an empire, like the carapace of a crab discarded on a beach by gulls. The Uttakin conquered Harkuna in ages past, but the lands of Golnir and Sokara that were once its vassal states still maintain the vestiges of ancient tradition. Harkuna remains the model of kingship even though the High King's Seat has been empty for three hundred years. Indeed, many superstitious folk still claim that the High King was never slain by the Uttakin, but sleeps under the frozen Rimewater and will arise when the World Snake spits fire and the end of the world looms.'

Those, at least, are the words of one long-dead author.

Turn to **368**.

699

'I believe I've encountered this isle before,' says the navigator, 'but it never shows up at exactly the place I last marked it on my charts.'

Put in at the island	turn to **682**
Sail on	turn to **283**

700

The crewmen are all dead, leaving you alone on your ship. You cannot sail her without help. In the rowboat it is possible you might be able to reach the mainland, but that would mean abandoning your cargo and supplies.

Put to sea in the rowboat	turn to **423**
Remain aboard the ship	turn to **518**

701

The fishermen entertain you and your men in their village tavern, but you suspect they may have spiked the ale because it is not long before the others are lolling drunkenly and singing ribald songs.

You have sensibly avoided drinking anything yourself, but now you must assert your authority to get the men back on board so you can set sail before the Reavers show up. Make a CHARISMA roll at a Difficulty of 14.

Successful CHARISMA roll	turn to **549**
Failed CHARISMA roll	turn to **378**

702

Lauria finally leaves the tavern, apparently well lubricated with Bluewood cider by now, and goes striding off into the fog singing to herself. To track her to her digs you must make a SCOUTING roll at Difficulty 14.

Successful SCOUTING roll	turn to **401**
Failed SCOUTING roll	turn to **477**

703

'Correct,' says Talanexor, arching his eyebrows. 'Good guess.'

No wimpy maths questions for you. This is meant to be a magical duel, isn't it? You toss the Curse of the Creeping Entrails at him, swiftly following it with a puissant hex you learned off an old village witch when you were a toddler. Make a MAGIC roll at Difficulty 13 if you're a Mage, Difficulty 17 if you're any other profession.

Successful MAGIC roll	turn to **383**
Failed MAGIC roll	turn to **365**

704

You go ashore on Starspike Island. It is a barren wilderness of broken rocks covered in scarlet moss. The central pinnacle rises almost vertically like a pillar supporting the heavens. Your men flatly refuse to try to scale it. As one man says, `I went to sea to become a sailor, not a mountaineer.'

Try to climb the mountain	turn to **695**
Set sail	turn to **230**

705

You follow a convoluted path that eventually brings you to the edge of the Bluewood. Increase your SCOUTING score by 1.

Go into Dweomer	turn to **571**
Go to the harbour	turn to **100**

706

You spend a pleasant few days on the Island of Fire. `Ah, 'tis an earthly paradise,' declares the first mate, sucking milk from a coconut while he is fanned by two lovely island maidens.

You suck your teeth, thinking that perhaps you'd better get your men back to sea before their discipline atrophies altogether.

Recover 2-12 Stamina if wounded and then turn to **479**.

707

The sailmaster is not popular with anyone on board. His protests of innocence fall on deaf ears. You order him trussed up and bundled overboard like a sack of food that had gone off.

Some days later, passing the mess, you overhear a conversation that you realize confirms the sailmaster's alibi. He could not possibly have committed the murder. You are filled with remorse. Get the codeword *Clanger* and turn to **188**.

708

The mixture explodes in your face. Cross the **selenium ore** off your list of possessions, then roll one die.

Score 1	You are killed; turn to **123**
Score 2-3	The hull is breached; turn to **486**
Score 4	Lose 1 from your MAGIC score; turn to **262**
Score 5-6	Lose 1-6 Stamina; turn to **262** if still alive

709

You are swept ashore at the mouth of a wide river. Nearby, impaled on the jagged end of a broken branch, a skeleton in rusting armour dangles at the water's edge. Apparently not all shipwrecked mariners are as lucky as you.

Searching the body, you find a **sword (COMBAT +1)**; add this to your list of possessions.

Staggering towards trails of smoke that are rising from beyond a copse of olive-green tropical palms, you arrive at a settlement of many thatched-roofed shacks raised on stilts at the river's edge. It is the depot town of Smogmaw, on the great southern continent.

Turn to **44**.

710

The harbourmaster studies your documents, which confirm you as owner of a small barque called the Thaumaturge. She has a carrying capacity of 1 Cargo Unit and her Crew Quality is average. Remember to change the entry in the Docked column each time you arrive at a new port; the Thaumaturge is currently docked at Dweomer, of course.

Cross off the **ship's deeds** and turn to **100**.

711

One night, hearing a commotion on deck, you come up from your cabin to find the sailors crowded along the rail. They are pointing into the water with cries of awe. Pushing your way through to the front, you are astonished to see the glittering lights of an undersea city shining up from below.

'I've heard tales of such a place,' says the first mate. 'It is the sunken city of Ys, cursed because its inhabitants blasphemed against the gods of the sea.'

Dive down to the city *Into the Underworld* **404**
Set a course away from here turn to **311**

712

There are only a few ships for sale and there is not much to choose between them. Choose from the types listed here.

Type	Cost	Capacity
Barque	240 Shards	1 Cargo Unit
Brigantine	500 Shards	2 Cargo Units

You get to give your ship a name. Record this and other details on your Ship's Manifest. The Crew Quality is poor.

Each time you arrive at a destination, change the entry in the Docked column on the Ship's Manifest to the ship's new location. Currently your ship is docked at Smogmaw, of course.

Now turn to **71**.

713

At last you manage to break free of the magic that has held you frozen. You cannot tell how much time has passed, but there is no sign of the Gorgons now.

Turn to **449**.

714

You are washed up on a narrow stretch of beach at the back of a bay surrounded by high mist-shrouded peaks.

A bottle has been swept up on to the shingle beside you. Though your fingers are trembling with cold, you manage to unscrew it. Inside you find a **ship's deeds**, which you can add to your list of possessions.

After resting to recover your strength, you pick your way up a series of steep paths until you can get a clear view of the island. To the north lies an expanse of glittering blue forest, so there can be no question where you are – Braelak, the Sorcerers' Isle. Nearer at hand is a tower built of obsidian blocks.

Enter the forest   turn to **697**
Go to the tower   turn to **426**

715

The gypsies offer you cash for any of the following items, if you have them and are willing to trade.

Item	To sell
Rope	20 Shards
Lantern	60 Shards
Candle	5 Shards
Water flask	20 Shards
Coral-red tresses	500 Shards
Golden katana	3000 Shards
Smoulder fish	90 Shards
Cross-staff (SCOUTING +2)	500 Shards
Violin	50 Shards
Parrot	90 Shards
Fishing hook	2 Shards
Boar's tusk	75 Shards
Green gem	100 Shards

When you have finished your business, if you have enough money to pay the gypsies the 100 Shards they want for cutting you out of the seaweed, turn to **50**. If not, turn to **570**.

716

You push up, dislodging the iron cover which falls aside with a clang. Emerging, you find yourself on a mist-swaddled street where high-towered edifices loom on all sides like phantom titans.

At the end of the alley you come across a man in a thick fur cape who is locking up his shop for the night. When you say you are lost, he points along the street to where a large latticed window gleams with mist-blurred lamplight. 'This is Dweomer. Yonder is the west window of Maudlin College.'

Turn to **508**.

717

The ship's water barrels are all empty. Some of the crew turn to drinking seawater in desparation, but this is no use – it only hastens the inevitable end. Turn to **123**.

718

The ship is swept far out to sea. Men and goods are washed overboard by crashing, ink-dark waves that snap your hawsers like twine.

Lose 1 Cargo Unit (if you have any cargo) and reduce your crew quality by one step – i.e. an excellent crew becomes good, a good crew becomes average, and an average crew becomes poor.

At last the storm blows itself out. You are left drifting in unknown waters.

Turn to **245**.

Adventure Sheet

NAME

PROFESSION

GOD

RANK

DEFENCE

ABILITY   SCORE

CHARISMA

COMBAT

MAGIC

SANCTITY

SCOUNTING

THIEVERY

STAMINA

When unwounded

Current:

POSSESSIONS (maximum of 12)

RESURRECTION ARRANGEMENTS

MONEY

TITLES and HONOURS

BLESSINGS

Codewords

☐ Cacogast	☐ Chance	☐ Clanger	☐ Cruel
☐ Calcium	☐ Cheese	☐ Clutch	☐ Cull
☐ Callid	☐ Cheops	☐ Colour	☐ Curdle
☐ Cancel	☐ Chill	☐ Coracle	☐ Cushat
☐ Catalyst	☐ Church	☐ Cosy	☐ Cutlass
☐ Cenotaph	☐ Cithara	☐ Covet	☐ Cyclops
☐ Certain	☐ Citrus	☐ Crag	☐ Cynosure
☐ Cerumen	☐ Civil	☐ Crocus	

Ship's Manifest

SHIP TYPE	NAME	CREW QUALITY	CARGO CAPACITY	CURRENT CARGO	WHERE DOCKED

OLD HARKUNA
GOLNIR
SOKARA
DRUID'S ISLE
MARLOCK CITY
RINGHORN
WISHPORT
YELLOWPORT
DRAGON ISLAND
CITTAKS
GRENDEL'S HALL
METRICIANS
AKU
DWEOMER
THE UNNUMBERED ISLE'S — THERE ARE REAVERS →
THE ISLAND OF FIRE
SORCERER'S ISLE
THE VIOLET OCEAN
BRAZEN
COPPER ISLAND
STARSPIKE ISLAND
SEA OF HYDRAS
THE INNIS SHOALS
SMOGMAW
THE SLEEPING ISLE
THE WEEPING JUNGLE

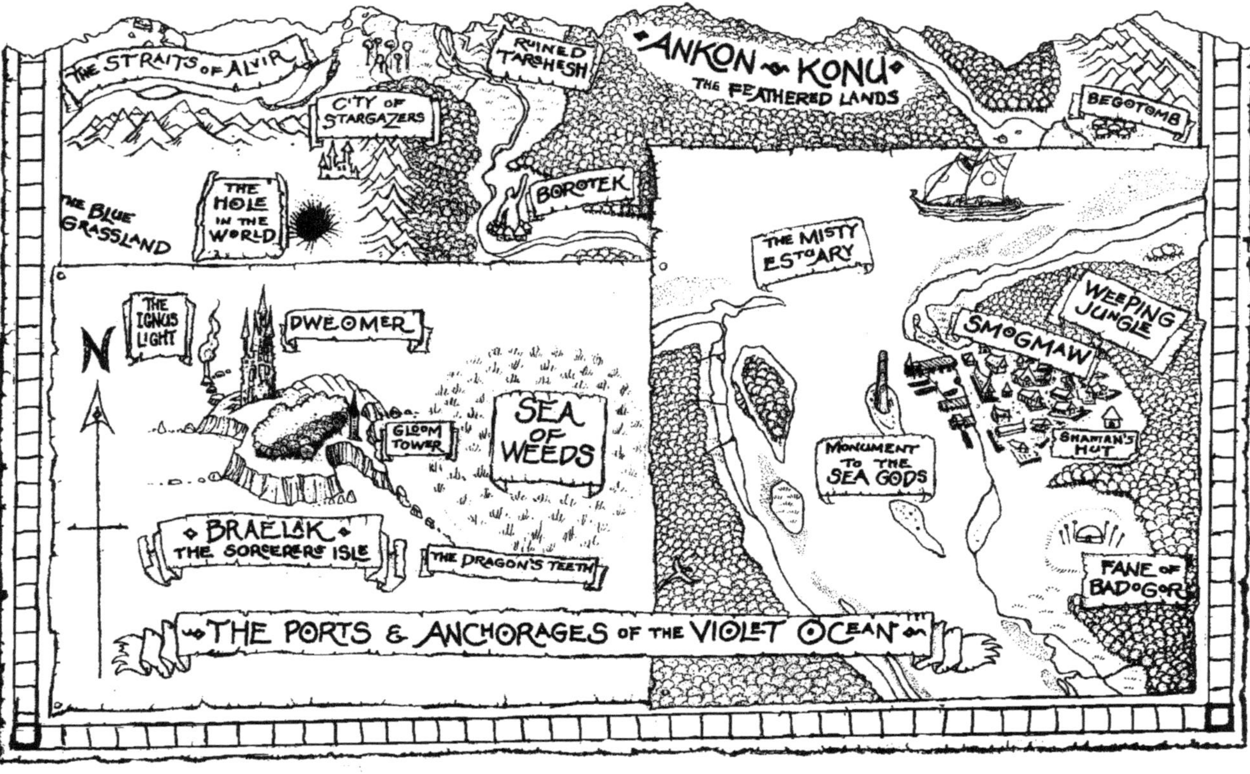

THE STRAITS OF ALVIR
CITY OF STARGAZERS
RUINED TARSHESH
ANKON-KONU
THE FEATHERED LANDS
BEGOTOMB
THE BLUE GRASSLAND
THE HOLE IN THE WORLD
BOROTEK
THE MISTY ESTUARY
WEEPING JUNGLE
SMOGMAW
SHAMAN'S HUT
THE IGNUS LIGHT
DWEOMER
GLOOM TOWER
SEA OF WEEDS
MONUMENT TO THE SEA GODS
N
BRAELAK
THE SORCERERS' ISLE
THE DRAGON'S TEETH
FANE OF BADOGOR
THE PORTS & ANCHORAGES OF THE VIOLET OCEAN